THE SISTERS OF KESTREL CAY

A SUMMER ISLE NOVEL

KELLY UTT

STANDARDS
OF STARLIGHT

2020 Standards of Starlight Paperback Edition

www.standardsofstarlight.com

ISBN: 978-1-952893-07-0

Cover art by Elizabeth Mackey

PART I

THE ISLANDS

1

FAMILY TIES

MARGOT

I'm sitting at my desk, sipping my morning coffee from an insulated paper cup when the phone rings. It's summertime, but the weather here in Washington State is cool and dreary. A far cry from the hot Florida summers of my youth, that's for sure. On the plus side, the views are stunning. My office has a large window that looks out over the Puget Sound. I haven't spotted any yet, but I've been told that humpback whales and orcas frequent these parts. I intend to keep an eye to the water so I might see the majestic creatures for myself.

I don't get many calls at work. When I do, I automatically suspect that it's Grandpa Vern. He likes talking on a landline for some old-fashioned reason. He rarely uses a mobile phone or contacts me on mine. It's one of his countless quirks. The man is in his late eighties now. I suppose by the time you get to that age, you've earned the right to do things the way you want.

I turn, straighten my back, and glance out into the row of cubicles in the distance to gauge whether I'll be able to have a personal conversation without being disturbed. No one is moving around out there, so I stand and close my door. Then I pick up the receiver, careful not to displace any strands of hair that have been neatly tied at the back of my head. Regulations say women's hair has to be off the collar, and with my thick, wavy locks, the bun takes forever to get right.

"Naval Air Station Whidbey Island. Ensign Callaway speaking," I say as I touch the phone to my ear.

Pride buoys me as I announce my post and rank.

"Margot?" his voice is scratchy on the other end of the line, but it's him.

"Grandpa Vern?" I reply, my voice rising.

"I'm here!" he says. "It's me, all the way from sunny Hideaway Isle, Florida. How are you, Little M?"

Little M is a nickname Grandpa has called me for as long as I can remember. I'm not sure why he started, or more importantly, why it lasted beyond my preschool years. I haven't been a little girl for a long time. A rush of embarrassment washes over me and I feel my cheeks fill with color. I take another glance out my office window to see if anyone is watching. Thankfully, they're not.

Deep down, it feels good when Grandpa uses the special name. It's one of the few remaining connections to a time in my life when I still believed that the world was a friendly and safe place. Hearing his familiar voice makes me cry, though. And I can't do that here.

"I'm good. I think the new assignment will suit me," I reply. "Even though I'm in the Pacific Northwest, being on an island makes it feel a little more like home."

Tears sting the edges of my eyes. I hide my head and

wipe them away, glad to have chosen waterproof mascara during my last trip to the drug store makeup aisle.

"Our girl, the Naval Officer," he says affectionately.

I love Grandpa Vern. The fact that he continues to love me when I'm not so easy to love only makes me feel more strongly for him. He's a good man. The kind that doesn't let you down, no matter what. I feel badly for pushing him away, especially after all he's done.

"Who would have thought?" I ask. "It's a far cry from where I started. Sometimes, it's hard to believe this is real."

"Nah," he replies, and I can almost see him wrinkling up his face, his bald head adjusting in sync. "You can do anything you set your mind to, Margot Callaway. You know that. You've *always* known that."

I nod because he's right. I'm a fighter. A survivor. Many others would have crumpled under the pressure. Not me.

I'm a bonafide Naval Flight Officer now. I've just been assigned to a squadron after eighteen months of flight training in Pensacola. I'm charged with leading a group of enlisted personnel and overseeing the squadron's operations. That includes things like administration, personnel management, and aircraft maintenance. I'm still getting my feet wet, but I'm proud of what I've made of myself.

I think Grandpa Vern is proud, too, that I graduated from the Naval Academy and have made a career in the military. He's said as much, although I tend to deflect praise instead of letting his words sink in. It's as if I'm still punishing myself for what happened, all these years later. Isn't that the way for a hard ass to handle things?

Annapolis, Maryland, where the Academy is located, was quite a distance from our home on Hideaway Isle in South Florida, yet Grandpa probably would have made the trip north to attend my graduation ceremony. I didn't want that to happen, so I didn't mention it until after the fact. Maybe once I get settled into my new position, I'll allow him a visit. Only my current station in Washington State is an even farther trip from South Florida than Annapolis was.

"Thanks, Grandpa," I say. "How's the weather down there?"

Small talk is important. It steers the exchange away from more sensitive matters.

"It's bright and gorgeous," he replies. "Warm, but not too warm to suit me. The water is sparkling and the birds are singing, just like every other day. There's no place else like our little slice of paradise. I'll stand by that claim until the day that I die."

"I'm glad you're happy there," I reply.

Every topic of conversation seems to volley past small talk and turn against me. I read into Grandpa's words, taking in the subtle digs, whether he intends them that way or not. It's as if he and I can't speak to each other without stirring old hurts. They're what bind us. I know he wishes I'd come back home, even just for a visit. I simply won't do that. I have to stay away. My sanity depends on it. I know he also wishes I'd talk to my sister.

"Little M," Grandpa Vern says slowly and deliberately, probably for dramatic effect. "Your mom and dad would be so proud of you."

His words hit me like a punch to the gut. I can't stop the tears now, despite my efforts to suck it up and hold them in. I reach for the paper towel I have wrapped around an apple and stashed in a drawer. Carefully, I loosen the absorbent fabric and blot my eyes with it, then I set the fruit on the top of my desk. I make a mental note to bring in a box of tissues. Or to stop taking calls from Grandpa Vern while I'm at work. Maybe if I get a landline phone connected at my new apartment in Oak Harbor, he'll call me there instead.

"I... I know," I reply, sputtering. "Thanks for saying so."

Mention of my parents brings it all rushing back, pain as fresh as ever.

My dad's been gone since I was in grade school, killed in a boating accident. It was horrible to lose him, but it happened out on the water and away from my uninitiated eyes. Mom's accident, on the other hand, was witnessed up close and personal. The scene plays like a movie in my mind, always queued up and ready for me to relive in vivid color.

I was nineteen and Lottie was twelve when Mom was hit. Her body didn't look like a body when I saw it just minutes after the impact. Instead, it looked like chunks of meat strewn around on the asphalt and ready to cook in the hot Florida sun. The image is burned into my memory like a tattoo, painful and permanent. I wish I could have been literally anywhere else in the world at that moment. It changed me, and not for the better.

We lived on the mainland then. I was a freshman at the University of Miami studying music performance. I wasn't sure what I'd do with the degree had I finished it, but I'd been offered a full scholarship to play the oboe, and so, took a chance. Grandpa Vern had made it easy by graciously allowing me to occupy a three-bedroom condo he owned in Coral Gables. Mom and Lottie had needed a place to stay, too, so my first college experience became a family affair. I didn't mind, most of the time. Mom wasn't the overbearing type. I had plenty of freedom to do my own thing. I spent the majority of my time on campus, anyway, practicing in the music building or performing in one of the countless ensembles required of me as a scholarship recipient.

The smell of handsy frat boys who hadn't quite figured out how to reapply deodorant comes rushing back as I glance at my diploma on the wall. I finished my degree, but not at the University of Miami, and not in music performance. The Naval Academy was an unexpected detour.

I'm a sensitive type by nature. As such, oboe suited me. I felt at home on stage, wearing one of my many long, elegant black dresses and sitting on the edge of a firm chair with my instrument to my lips. If I close my eyes, I can still hear the orchestra plodding away around me as the downbeat reverberates throughout my chest. I enjoyed being part of something bigger than my singular voice. Music was my respite.

Bach was my favorite. I'll never forget the solo I played in "Jesu, Joy of Man's Desiring" at Christmas with both the chorale and orchestra accompanying. My entire being came alive that evening as the group of us slowly and reverently performed the piece together. The auditorium was packed. Everyone in attendance was mesmerized by the glorious sounds filling the room. I can still feel the warmth of the spotlight on my skin, the tiny particles of dust visible as they floated through the air. I was born to be in that spotlight. I soaked it up like a sapling in the sun.

Seeing my mom's accident changed all of that. I was forced to toughen up. Life is a bitch who left me no choice in the matter.

"Keep it together, Margot Callaway," Life breathed in my ear as I lay in bed at night, unable to sleep. "No use dwelling on things after the fact. What's done is done."

Some details of Mom's accident are fuzzy. Others are crystal clear. Mom had been riding her bicycle on Patcher Road that bright April afternoon. She was in the bicycle lane, dutifully wearing her Consumer Product Safety Commission-approved helmet. She had reflectors in all the right places. She knew how to share the road and signal her turns.

None of that mattered when a dump truck driver decided to make a sudden left into a gas station. He ran Mom down, apparently, without even noticing. He dragged her body— what was left of it, anyway— more than thirty feet.

I'll never forget the wet mark she left on the pavement. Until then, I hadn't realized a human body had so much liquid in it. Or maybe what I hadn't realized was what all that liquid would look like once a body was burst wide open.

It's gruesome, I know. As strange as it sounds, something about the mechanics of it all provides me comfort. The rote details help me remain distanced. If I go over Mom's death in the coldest, most rudimentary terms, I can keep moving forward. Otherwise, I might fall apart. It's been almost seven years. In many ways, it feels like yesterday. Isn't that the way it always goes with trauma?

Lottie still cries for her. I'm privy to this fact not because my little sister shares her personal life with me or because I'm around to hear her sobs in person. No, I'm too far away for either-- physically *and* emotionally. I know it because Grandpa Vern tells me during our telephone conversations. He would love to see me and for us to talk more often. I'm the one who keeps him at arm's length, close enough to feel connected yet far enough to become ensnared by the hurts of the past.

Sometimes I miss Grandpa and Lottie, something fierce. They don't realize it, but I often cry for them, too, when I cry for Mom. I'd love nothing more than to eat fried ham and cheese sandwiches-- our favorite!-- with Grandpa. Or to discuss with my sister the latest J.K. Rowling novel and what's happening in Stan Lee's Marvel universe. The two of us used to be more than just sisters. We were friends. Close friends, despite our seven-year age difference. But to do any of those things would mean going back to the place where my trauma happened. The only way I know how to deal with the pain is to keep moving, and to stay away.

"Margot, doll," Grandpa says after I've been quiet on the line for too long. "Are you still there?"

"Yes, I'm here," I say, collecting myself.

"Good. Because there's something important I need to talk to you about. Something has... well, something has happened..."

2

ARM'S LENGTH

I've had all I can take for the moment. I can't do this here. I won't. I have a job to perform, and I'm not about to damage my reputation when my colleagues are still getting to know me.

Personal issues will have to wait. They must be handled privately.

I make an excuse about someone needing me and I move to end the call with Grandpa Vern abruptly. I promise to get back to him as soon as I can, but I tell him I'm swamped with work and it might be a while. He doesn't object, and that's the saddest part. He's used to me brushing him off. I'm worried, though. It sounded like, this time, he may have had something serious to tell me. I wonder what. I meander through a list of potential possibilities in my mind, but stop when I decide nothing good will come from speculating.

No one actually needs me right now, so I pull my mobile phone out and call my closest friend.

Chevelle Mooney and I have been thick as thieves

since first grade. She's the only person from Hideaway Isle besides Grandpa Vern that I keep in touch with. She still lives on the island, employed as a school counselor at Turngate Elementary. Chevelle and I have an arrangement. She comes to visit me a couple times a year wherever I am, or else we meet someplace swanky for a long weekend every few months. She doesn't ask me to return to Hideaway Isle. She never would. She gets it.

I smooth the front of my uniform while I wait for my friend to answer. She picks up on the second ring.

"Chevelle?"

"Margot, my dear! What's up?" she replies in an enthusiastic whisper.

I hear her heels clink on the tile floor, then the sound of her office door creaking as she closes it. She's at work, too.

I get right down to business.

"Grandpa Vern called a few minutes ago. He said he has something important to tell me… that something has happened…"

I hear more tapping. Her fingernails on her desk this time. I'll bet she's wearing a colorful outfit and bold accessories that look fabulous against her dark skin. Chevelle has always been more of a girly girl than me. She dresses to the nines every single work day. She'd never make it in the military without her adornments. I chuckle as I look down at my drab uniform. It wouldn't suit the marvelous Ms. Mooney. For me, though, it's fine.

Every once in a while, I miss dressing up for oboe concerts and feel the urge to put on something fancy. The impulse doesn't last long. I typically get it out of my system when Chevelle and I meet up. She encourages me to dress nicely on at least a portion of whatever adventures we undertake, and she makes sure to build the perfect outing into our schedule.

We're planning to get together for the upcoming Fourth of July holiday, although we haven't settled on a location yet. We'd better get busy sorting that out. The Fourth is less than a month away. I'm thinking somewhere on the water where there's a good-sized Independence Day celebration. I have enough leave stored up to spend a whole week away if I want to. Chevelle has quite a bit of time off this summer, so she ought to be able to stay as long as I can.

Charleston, South Carolina maybe? I hear they throw a great party at Patriots Point, next to the USS Yorktown. Or perhaps New York City. I was there for the Fourth once. There's nothing quite like celebrating our nation's independence with the Statue of Liberty visible in the distance. I don't think Chevelle has ever been to New York. I could suggest a visit to the 9/11 Memorial & Museum in keeping with the patriotic theme of the trip. That kind of thing means an awful lot to me now that I'm in the Navy. I'd like to share more of it with my best friend. Not to mention, there are plenty of reasons to dress up for a night out in the Big Apple. Maybe we'll even meet the men of our dreams. Neither of us are dating anyone. We'd like that to change.

Chevelle pulls me out of my daydream and back to the matter at hand.

"You want me to do some digging and see what I can find out?" she asks.

"Would you?"

"Done," she replies.

"Thanks, Chevelle. You're the best."

She doesn't say anything else right away. I hear furious typing on her keyboard and the fast clicking of her mouse, followed by the tapping of her pencil, probably on her desk. Chevelle knows Grandpa Vern nearly as well as I do. She can predict what he might be up to.

"Are you Googling?" I ask.

"Mm hmm," she mumbles.

Why didn't I think of that? Leave it to Chevelle to take the straightest route to solving a problem. She is insanely efficient. And she's smart as a whip. If something serious has happened in Grandpa Vern's world, there's a good chance the news has spread around the island by now. Nothing stays quiet there for long. Chevelle is probably scouring the internet for clues. First the local paper, then social media. If nothing turns up there, she can check in with her various contacts on the police force and at the courthouse.

Chevelle earned both her bachelor's and master's degrees at the University of Miami, but returned home to Hideaway Isle immediately after graduation. Her connections are her biggest strength. I'm sometimes jealous of how at home she feels on our little island. It's as if she was meant to spend her life there, gradually growing old while wrapped securely in the warm, tropical breeze, her friends and loved ones bustling around her cheerfully. All except for me. I'm the friend she has to travel to visit with. I wish I felt such a strong connection to the place. To any place, for that matter.

"Find anything?" I ask.

I could search, too, but I wouldn't want to use military

computers or internet networks for the task. Besides, Chevelle is on the case.

"Working on it," she says. Then, cautiously, "Did he mention anything about Lottie?"

I grimace. I hoped this wouldn't be about her. My guilt at leaving my little sister alone with Grandpa is off the charts. Especially after she confided in me about what she was going through before Mom's accident ever happened.

Lottie needed me. I knew that. She was struggling to find her footing as a preteen. Middle school was miserable, complete with fake friends and shameless bullies. Each day was a minefield that sweet, naive Lottie wasn't equipped to successfully navigate. I stood ready and willing to play the protective big sister role, until my world came crashing down and I had to save myself. Like on an airplane, the way they tell you to put your oxygen mask on first before assisting others in the event of a crash. I had to reach for a lifeline of my own.

I exhale loudly before I answer.

"He didn't," I reply. "More like, I didn't give him a chance. It was rude of me, Chevelle. I cut the poor man off before he could tell me whatever it is he wants to say. And he just stopped talking, like he knew I'd withdraw. I feel terrible about the way I handled it."

She taps her pencil some more, no doubt considering how much to tell me. I assume that Chevelle sees Lottie and Grandpa Vern from time to time. Maybe even regularly-- at the grocery store, in line at the bank, or out to dinner at one of the local restaurants. There are so many tourists to weave through that permanent residents can usually spot each other quickly in a crowd. It's a survival mechanism of sorts. Chevelle doesn't mention it.

"Margot, I don't want to get in the middle of your family's business," she says. And now I know she found something.

"Spill it," I say.

"Okay, then, see for yourself," she instructs. "Lottie's social media. It's public. At least, a lot of it is. I'm looking at Facebook right now."

I raise a hand to my forehead and stroke it gently, like an infant trying to self sooth. The idea of looking at my sister's Facebook profile makes me physically ill. I haven't seen Lottie's face all these years. Although, I admit that I've wondered what she'd look like, an adult of nineteen now. In a strange symmetry, she's the age I was when Mom died.

Sometimes, when I can't sleep at night, I see Lottie's face in the darkness, its smooth edges having sharpened with time. When I do sleep, she haunts my dreams. I see her with Mom, smiling and happy, then alone and devastated. The dreams take many forms. The particulars are different, but the progression is always the same. I wake up in a cold sweat, marinating in shame over leaving her like I did.

"Chev, that's…"

"I hear you," she replies. "You know I understand as well as anyone could. But if you want to learn what Grandpa Vern is talking about, I think you need to see it for yourself."

"Ugh. Do I have to?"

"Unless you're going to call him back and ask," she says, wisely.

I lean my head to one side, then the other. I feel like a caged animal looking for an escape. How cruel Life is, to chase me down no matter how far I run. What constitutes a safe distance? How do I escape?

"Is it that serious?" I ask.

Chevelle pauses, choosing her words carefully. "Let's just say it might finally be time for you to make a trip home. The Fourth is coming up… You can stay with me…"

Beads of perspiration form on my brow at the thought of it. Staying with Chevelle would be okay, but returning to Hideaway Isle would most certainly not. It would be torture. Not to mention, I want to do something fun for the Fourth. Haven't I suffered enough? I deserve to have fun. I deserve to be free from the burdens of my family. I deserve some semblance of peace.

"Have you lost your ever loving mind?" I ask my friend.

I turn to my keyboard, and I'm the one typing furiously now. I'm annoyed. The emotion needs an outlet before it turns to rage. Or worse, panic. My heart pounds against my ribs. I no longer care who from my squadron views my internet search or overhears my conversation. I'm a ball of hurt feelings. My wounded psyche has been activated. The pain threatens to pour out of me.

"Easy, girl," Chevelle says, as if she's talking to a wild horse. Her tone only irritates me further. "What are you typing? Are you navigating to Facebook?"

"No," I say sternly, doing my best to keep my voice down. "I'm going to mother fucking Google Maps. I want to know the exact distance between Hideaway Isle and Whidbey Island. Just to, you know, confirm that being across the fucking country isn't far enough. I should have accepted that duty assignment in Germany. Although, hell, the flight times are probably similar."

Chevelle is silent as I type locations into the mapping program. She knows to handle me with kid gloves when I get like this. There's no reasoning with me. I hate myself for it, but I'm powerless to reign it in. I grab the apple from the top of my desk and squeeze it like a stress ball. The fruit's skin tenses under the pressure.

"The distance is more than three thousand miles," I say. "Between my island and yours. *Three thousand*, Chev! And it isn't far enough. Can you believe that shit? My bullshit past follows me. I can't get away. I want so badly to get away."

I hear muffled voices on the other end of the line. It sounds like Chevelle is talking to someone. Like she has the phone leaned against an item of clothing. I take the opportunity to breathe deeply in an effort to calm down. I remind myself that Chevelle is at her place of employment. The kids are out for the summer, but faculty and staff are working another couple of weeks. Chevelle is a professional. I can't be interrupting her and inserting my family drama like this. I end the call, sending her a quick text.

I'm sorry, Chev. Call you later.

Once I'm no longer seeing red, I go to my commander and inform him that there's a family emergency I need to tend to. He tells me to take the rest of the day off, so I do. Thankfully, he doesn't ask questions. I'm not sure how I would have answered them if he had.

In typical Pacific Northwest fashion, it drizzles as I

drive from the air base to my apartment in nearby Oak Harbor. The white Subaru Outback I purchased when I moved here last month hums along, gripping the curvy roads resolutely, eager to please. It's the first new car I've ever owned. I chose white because I thought it would be a nice contrast against the deep greens of the dense forest and the deep blues of the sea. And besides, white looks good with my new Washington State license plate on the back. The car is a reminder that I'm a full grown adult now. No one can tell me what to do unless they're my superior in the Navy. No one can gain control over my life unless I voluntarily give it to them.

If only I felt like an adult when it came to my family and my past. That'd be great. Wouldn't it?

3

MERCY

L ottie was an easy baby from the start. Mom had her
at home with the help of a Jamaican midwife. The
labor went smoothly, barely lasting four hours. I was there
when my sister was born, camped out on a sleeping bag
in a corner of my parents' bedroom. I still remember
what little Lottie Marcella looked like moments after
making her entrance into the world, all squishy skin and
thick blonde hair. Her middle name, Marcella, was
selected as a nod to Mars, the Roman god of fertility,
because Mom had been told she couldn't have any more
babies. It took her a while, but I guess she proved them
wrong.

My kid sister was a big baby, weighing nearly nine
pounds. She was strong, too. She immediately took to
Mom's breast and nursed like a little pink piggy. I
remember Mom and Dad remarking that I had been
smaller and less vivacious as a newborn. Whatever that
meant. I didn't know what they were talking about, at the

time. It didn't matter much. I was a happy six-year-old with a new baby sister and a seventh birthday coming up.

Life was good then. At least, as far as I knew. A slew of friends and family members doted on me and baby Lottie, including Grandpa Vern.

Oh, how I wish we could go back to that place in time. Mom and Dad were alive, our existence was simple, and Lottie had every opportunity ahead of her. Our needs were met, and we were loved. I don't think any of us had an idea how drastically our luck would turn. If we had known what despair and destruction awaited us, I'm sure we would have somehow shifted gears and changed course. Sadly, it's far too late for that now.

As Lottie matured into a bouncing baby and then a curious toddler, our seven year age difference didn't keep us apart. To the contrary, I was like a second mother, making sure she was entertained with silly songs, fed with healthy snacks, and tucked in at night with bedtime stories. I enjoyed taking care of my baby sister. I enjoyed *having* a baby sister. I was proud to show her off to everyone I knew. But it went farther than that. I had the distinct sense that Lottie and I had known each other before. I couldn't say when or where. I'm not even sure what I believe when it comes to such matters of the human spirit. But I just knew we belonged together. Like peas and carrots. It was Margot and Lottie, Lottie and Margot. The Callaway sisters.

If you'd asked me back then whether my sister and I could ever grow apart and spend seven years not speaking to each other, I'd have said you were crazy. It would have seemed an impossibility. Yet, here we are. With each day that passes, bridging the gap between us becomes more difficult. I'm honestly not sure our relationship can be salvaged. I fear it's too far gone. Or maybe it's that I'm too far gone, three thousand miles away in Washington State. I'm nearly in Canada, for Christ's sake.

When I arrive at my apartment complex, I stop at the mail center. There aren't many people who know my new address, but it seems like I should check the box in case there's something important in there. There isn't. I slowly meander, admiring the evergreens that have been artfully placed around the property. It's true, I love the landscape. It's so different from home in Florida, and really, from anywhere I've ever lived before. But if I'm being honest with myself, I'm dragging my feet and wishing to do almost anything besides what I know I must. After a casual stroll in the precipitation that has now become a cool, fine mist, I force myself to get home and focused.

I walk the three flights of stairs to my unit and enter with my key. I step inside, then shrug off my flight suit the minute the door is closed behind me. It's freeing to strip down to my undergarments and the thin black t-shirt I wear underneath my uniform. I walk to my bedroom and rummage through a drawer until my hands find a pair of soft yoga pants. My favorites. I slip them on, reveling in their smooth decadence, then I find my plush pink slippers in the closet and slide my feet into them.

I try to appreciate the little things. Being home to enjoy these comforts in the middle of the afternoon is a special treat.

I haven't fully furnished my place yet. A pang of loneliness hits me as I look around at the sparse decor and take in the deep silence. The dreary weather outside makes for dim lighting indoors. It seems all wrong for it to be this dreary in June. I must find a way to brighten the space somehow. The silence has its benefits, but I miss the bustling energy of my Florida home. There's something about a tropical climate and the views to go along with it that lends itself to festivities and human connection.

If I had gone down a different path in life-- if Mom hadn't been killed-- I'd probably be living on Hideaway Isle right now. I would have finished my music performance degree at the University of Miami, and if I'd been lucky, I would have secured a spot in our island's philharmonic orchestra. Even though the island is small, the tourism economy supports a world class orchestra. Back when I was a music student, I hadn't come up with any firm plans for after college graduation. But I think that deep down, a career in music at home on Hideaway Isle is what I envisioned for myself.

Maybe I would have taught music to children on the side. Even though my concentration in college was performance, I've always nurtured a soft spot for music education. Wouldn't that have been grand? Chevelle and I, working at the same elementary school? If given the chance, my best friend and I would probably hang out together most days after work. Maybe we'd be roommates. I can imagine us, joined at the hip and savoring every single good thing about island life. Isn't that what best friends are supposed to do while in their twenties? Until they get married and start families, anyway.

I admit, the idea has its charm.

I sigh and turn my attention back to the present. Now that I'm assigned to a squadron, maybe I should get a cat. Or maybe even a dog, so long as I find someone to keep the creature when I'm out of town on assignment. In this age and with the ever expanding gig economy, finding a trustworthy pet sitter shouldn't be hard to do. Especially if I get a small or medium sized dog. I hear that larger breeds are harder to find good caretakers for.

Lottie and I owned cats growing up. And not just common variety cats. Many of the felines on Hideaway Isle are polydactyl, having extra toes on their paws that look like mittens the same way the famous Hemingway cats in Key West do. Our plump tabby, affectionately named Butterball, had extra toes on both front paws. His extra toes were symmetrical. They looked like opposable thumbs. I'd love to have another kitty like him.

The Hemingway connection is fascinating. Historians at the Hemingway Home and Museum claim Ernest Hemingway was given a white six-toed cat by a ship's captain. They say that some of the cats who live on the museum grounds are descendants of that original cat, who was named Snow White. I'm only speculating, but it makes sense that the polydactyl cats on our island stem from the same blood line. Our close proximity to Key West makes the shared lineage likely, in my mind.

I lower myself onto the new extra-deep beige sofa that was delivered less than a week ago. I haven't purchased decorative pillows to coordinate yet, but I'm pleased with my furniture choices so far. I'm all about comfort whenever possible. Chevelle jokes about my proclivity for what feels good over what looks nice. She'll say beige is boring, but I don't see anything wrong with it. I laugh as I think about her teasing me. Hopefully, she'll be able to come visit soon and razz me about my bland-looking, comfortable sofa in person. I doubt she'll have anything negative to say once she sits down and feels for herself how good it is. I make a mental note to find some colorful pillows before she arrives. I add it to the growing list of things I want to take care of in an effort to make Whidbey Island feel more like some sort of home.

I pop open my laptop and search for polydactyl kittens near me. It's a long shot, but I spend more than twenty minutes scouring various marketplace listings and classified ads. With each stroke of the keys, I realize that I'm working overtime to avoid looking at Lottie's Facebook page. It's remarkable just how far I'll go to dodge my responsibility to my sister. When I don't find any kittens with extra toes in the greater Seattle and Vancouver metro areas, I decide it's time to stop screwing around and face what awaits me.

I make a hasty trip to the bathroom to splash some cold water on my face, then I pour myself a glass of water from the pitcher I keep chilled in the fridge. I move my laptop to the bar-height countertop between the kitchen and dining areas in my apartment. For some reason, I feel better equipped to handle this standing up. Gathering all of my courage, I navigate to Facebook and type my sister's name into the white search bar that sits waiting on top of the site's familiar, tranquil blue: *Lottie Callaway*.

I hold my breath as I wait for her profile to appear. In less than a minute, there she is: *Lottie M. Callaway in Hideaway Isle, Florida*. I click on her profile picture to enlarge it. For the first time in what feels like forever, my sister stares back at me. Tears spring to my eyes as I exhale slowly. Seeing her is... well, it's actually a relief. I should have looked her up a long time ago.

Her face has changed. It's rounder in some places--

around the eyes and in the apples of her cheeks. It's more angular and refined in others. Her skin has a golden glow, kissed by the sun. She's pretty. She looks so much more like Mom than she used to. And like me. I'm in awe of the family resemblance the three of us share. It makes me feel a part of something bigger, whether I try to deny my inclusion in that something or not.

"Little Lottie," I say out loud. "You've gone and grown up."

Something about this fact makes me sad, as if my sister could have remained a child forever, frozen in time at the moment where I left her. How unfair would that have been? I know how unreasonable it sounds as I think it. Yet I can't hold back the tears that are now streaming down my cheeks indignantly. How dare I place any expectations on this young woman? I chose to leave and to cut myself out of her life. As such, I have no bearing on her future. Her decisions are not mine to weigh in on. Her life is hers alone. Things might have been different, but now, it is what it is. Too much time has passed for me to get involved. Whatever I learn, I won't overstep. I make that silent promise.

My God, this is hard.

It takes me a few minutes of reflection before I can move forward. My mood is somber. My connection to my sister is profound, even under the strained circumstances we find ourselves in.

Once I absorb the shock of observing Lottie's nineteen-year-old face and regain my composure, I dig deeper to find out what Chevelle saw on her Facebook profile. Hopefully, it's the same thing Grandpa Vern wanted to talk about. I intend to call him back as soon as I figure it out.

I gather my nerves and proceed, clicking through the popular sections on Lottie's profile: Overview, Places Lived, Contact and Basic Info. She has strict privacy settings in place. I can't garner much except that her current city is set to Hideaway Isle. Apparently, she hasn't gone away for college. I guess that's a bit of a surprise, although I wouldn't judge her if she decided that higher education isn't the right fit. College isn't for everyone.

I don't see what it is that Chevelle was referring to until, finally, I click on the Work and Education section. There, under Work, Lottie is listed as Owner at a company called Island Boat Tours.

I lower my brow and take my hands away from the keyboard. I'm shocked. This doesn't make sense. Lottie is a nineteen-year-old girl, apparently lacking in education beyond high school. How could she own a boat tour company? Unless she became some sort of child prodigy while I was away, it doesn't add up. Could she have made it up to look successful online? Or as a joke? Perhaps it's something people younger than me do these days. I tell myself to remain calm and not jump to conclusions. There has to be an explanation.

I reach for the laptop again, opening a new tab. I type the name of the boat company in carefully, then wait for the results. Almost immediately, I understand what alarmed Chevelle. The results are numerous. All include Lottie's name. The headline on top tells the story as well as any other. It reads: 15 killed in tour boat accident, teenage owner of company charged.

News of the boat accident is absolutely horrendous.

But that's not all. As I scroll lower and the search results expand, even stranger headlines make mention of Lottie having proclaimed psychic powers. My sister has said publicly that she can communicate with our dead mother, and that Mom is telling her what to do.

4

FRIENDLIES

"I'm coming home," I say when the call connects.

Grandpa Vern hasn't said hello. I hear the soft thump of his ceiling fan in the background. He hardly ever runs the air conditioner, preferring instead to sit in a shaded spot under a gentle breeze. I can see him now, perched on one of his rattan bar stools near the phone as he looks out the window of his open lanai to the bay below. He's been complaining about the mangroves that are beginning to block his water view. Apparently, they're protected and can't be trimmed.

"Did Chevelle tell you what's happening?" he asks.

"Sort of," I reply. "She encouraged me to look for myself, so I did a little internet research."

He's quiet, and I think I hear muffled sobs.

"Grandpa?"

"I'm here," he says. "Thank you, Margot, for coming home. You'll probably never realize how much this means to me. I've tried my hardest to raise Lottie right. She's... well, at times, she's a handful. She doesn't have the same steadiness that you do. She's saying and doing all the wrong things. She's in over her head."

"It sounds like it," I reply.

"I shouldn't say it that way," he continues, his voice breaking.

"What way?"

"I mean those words... *over her head*... after, you know... the accident on the water... those poor people..."

He's stumbling, tripping over his words. He sounds far more discombobulated than he did this morning. I wonder if something else has happened. Perhaps he's just overwhelmed to hear that I'm finally returning to Hideaway Isle. What choice do I have?

"It's okay, Grandpa. I know your heart," I say. "You don't have to explain your words to me."

He whelps, the emotion bursting out of him. "I keep going over it in my mind. I can imagine their terrified faces. It was a fire. The boat caught fire, trapping those people below deck."

"That's horrible," I say. "What a terrifying way to go."

"Authorities are saying crew and owner negligence were responsible... for those *deaths*... I can hardly wrap my mind around it," Grandpa muses. "Those people had lives. They had families. Now they're gone."

"Owning a boat tour company is a lot of responsibility," I say. "Every person who steps onto a boat operated by an American company trusts that they'll be safe. That's one of the things we value most in this country. Thanks to our regulatory agencies and safety laws, we shouldn't have to worry when we contract a business."

I think about my time spent in less developed countries. Even though I haven't been in the Navy for long since graduating from the Academy, I've had the opportunity to travel quite a bit. I've been to parts of Africa where the contrast to our American way of life is pronounced. Also, Chevelle and I have made several trips to Mexico and islands in the Caribbean where there isn't the same assurance of safety.

"I know! I'm sick over this," Grandpa says. "The tourists that come to Hideaway Isle to enjoy themselves expect they'll be safe. Those of us who live here must be good stewards, especially the business owners who invite those tourists in with promises of beach music, cold drinks, and the like. It's all fun and games until someone gets hurt. And now... fifteen people..."

My grandpa must be under a lot of pressure. I haven't spent much time considering it, but in many ways, Grandpa Vern has had a hard road to travel. I suddenly feel deeply for him. It's as if I see him as an individual now, for more than just the role he's played in my life.

Born not long after the Great Depression, Vernon Callaway came into a world mired in uncertainty. He was an only child, and times were tough for him growing up. Both of his working-class parents died when he was a young man. His father was killed in a manufacturing accident when Vern was seventeen, and his mother died of pneumonia when he was twenty-one. Grandpa always says he had the best parents, only they hadn't stuck around long enough. He knew his paternal grandparents, though they didn't last much longer. They both passed away of old age related maladies before Vern's twenty-third birthday.

The way he tells the story, those grandparents had been wealthy, even though no one knew it. They were sitting on a lot of money they hadn't told a soul about. Vern isn't even sure how they came into possession of their fortune. When they died, he was their sole heir. That sounds lucky, and I guess it was. But it was also overwhelming to a young man in his early twenties who saw himself as working class and had no idea how to manage that kind of wealth. So, he did what his grandparents had done. He squirreled it away and lived most of his life as if the money didn't exist. The strategy had its merits, but it wasn't without its dangers. We may be seeing the effects of those dangers playing out now, with Lottie's present troubles.

Vern married my grandma, Eloise, who he loved very much. Sadly, love wasn't enough to keep tragedy from striking again. Eloise died during childbirth while bringing their only child, my dad, Jon Callaway, into the world. Grandpa Vern never remarried. He never even dated, as far as I know. He claims Grandma Eloise was his one true love, and that he'll never replace her. He raised Dad on his own.

I can only imagine the heartache he felt when Dad was killed. At that point, Vern must have felt cursed. Most people would. He'd lost every single person close to him except his granddaughters, which is why he eagerly stepped in after Mom died and Lottie needed a caretaker. Hearing what Lottie is into now makes me feel a newfound camaraderie with Grandpa Vern. I might finally have a better understanding of why he wants so desperately for us all to get along and be together. He's learned the hard way that staying alive is the lion's share of the work in a family where tragedy seems inevitable. But staying sane and out of trouble is a mountain to climb, too. Not to mention, finding the happiness that so cruelly eludes us Callaways. With so few of us left and Lottie spinning out of control, we must band together.

"You're a good one, Little M," he says softly. "How soon can you get here?"

I look around at my sparsely furnished apartment, then out the window at the sad, gloomy weather. Nothing is keeping me here. I have plenty of leave available since I rarely use it. I have more than a week, if I want to take the time. My commander seemed supportive of my family issues. Feeling determined to return to Hideaway Isle and offer genuine help to Lottie and Uncle Vern, I decide to take a whole month. Less than an hour ago, I wouldn't have dreamed of doing such a thing. Now, it feels right.

"Let me talk to my commander," I say. "I don't expect any pushback. I'll ask for a month off. Thirty whole days. If things with Lottie aren't stabilized within that amount of time, I can ask for more. Once my commander approves my request, I'll get on the next flight to South Florida. I'm coming to help you, Grandpa Vern. You are not alone in this."

"Thank you, thank you, thank you," he says. "I just can't thank you enough, Margot. Truly."

"It's okay, Grandpa," I say. "You don't have to thank me. But I do have one question."

"Anything. Go ahead."

"Is Lottie really the owner of the boat tour company? At her age?"

He sighs heavily. So much exhaled air between the

two of us. It's as if we have to sigh to make it through the difficult moments we face.

"It's true. She's the owner."

I hate to ask a follow up question since I said just one question, but I must know.

"Did she use…?"

"Her inheritance, yes," he says, finishing my sentence. "She's using the money I gave her, and not wisely. I can't help but feel partially responsible for this mess."

The day Mom died, Grandpa Vern sat us down at the dining table in his modest condo and told us how much he was worth. Lottie and I were floored. I don't think either of our parents knew. At that time, Grandpa's total assets were north of twenty million. I'm sure his investments have grown in the years since. The market has been good, and Grandpa never touches the money. He doesn't live like a pauper, but he certainly isn't flaunting his wealth either. His condo is less than two thousand square feet and located in a middle class golf community for retirees. He drives a Honda minivan, which he still washes himself, by hand. He buys his clothes at T.J. Maxx and uses coupons for the lunch buffet at his favorite soup and salad place. To look at him, you'd never know he was wealthy.

That day, as we prepared for Mom's funeral, Grandpa Vern said he wanted us to know that we had solid ground under our feet. He told us that we shouldn't feel vulnerable or alone because he was there, and the money he'd inherited from his grandparents would be enough to go around. I still remember the feel of the sawgrass chairs sticking to my legs in the heat of the day and the smell of freshly-squeezed orange juice waiting untouched in glasses on the table in front of us. To our great surprise, Grandpa Vern gave us each one million to do with what we pleased, once we were eighteen. The rest, we'd inherit when he died unless there was a good reason to use it sooner.

Since I was nineteen at the time, I received my million right away. It did give me peace of mind, but I'm much like Grandpa in my desire to live a humble, down-to-earth life. I don't feel the need for a flashy existence focused on shallow pursuits and efforts to one-up the next rich prick. I invested the money I received in stocks, and by and large, I haven't thought twice about it. I keep a cushion in a money market account that affords me the luxury of extra evenings out with Chevelle when we get together. But otherwise, I'm following the family tradition of living humbly. Apparently, Lottie is making different choices.

"She got it when she turned eighteen?" I ask, already knowing the answer.

Grandpa is nothing if not equitable. Knowing that he gave me a million dollars, I can be certain that he gave Lottie the same when she was of age.

"Yes," Grandpa Vern replies. "It was what I'd promised. And it was only fair."

"I know, Grandpa. I know."

"I suspected Lottie wouldn't handle it as well as you had. I should have intervened. I should have done something."

"Does she still live with you?" I ask. I suspect not.

"No," he says, and I can hear the air slowly seep out of his body like the wind going out of sails. "She moved out on her own the day she turned eighteen. I tried to stop her, sort of... There wasn't... I..."

"Right."

"It's all such a mess. That's the only word for it. I'm beside myself."

"I get it. I'll be there soon," I say.

Grandpa Vern thanks me again, profusely, and I end the call. I promise to let him know as soon as my flight is booked and I'm on my way. I don't bother to ask about Lottie's supposed psychic powers and what she's told people regarding her claims of communicating with our deceased mom. I also don't bother to contact Lottie directly. What I have to say to her must be said in person. That will happen soon enough.

5

JOURNEY

Less than eight hours later, I'm on an airplane high above Middle America on my way to Miami. The flight is a red eye out of Seattle, where I left my new car in long term parking. Thankfully, the plane isn't very crowded. I buy a pillow and a blanket from the flight attendant and manage to get a few hours of sleep as we travel southeast to the Sunshine State.

When I'm not sleeping, my mind wanders in anticipation of what it will be like to return to my hometown after all these years away. I ruminate on everything from whether I'll run into Kip Campbell, my high school boyfriend, to how different things will look thanks to the new construction projects Grandpa has told me about. I do my best to put any negative thoughts on hold in favor of focusing on the positive. I'll take things one step at a time.

As much as I hate to admit it, I'm excited. Maybe deep down, I wanted to return home. I don't think I would have done it on my own without a compelling reason. I hope I'm not speaking too soon, but perhaps by the time this is all over, I'll be grateful to Lottie for bringing me back.

We land at Miami International Airport in South Florida a few minutes past seven the following morning, local time. From there, I take a commuter flight to Hideaway Isle, where Chevelle is waiting for me.

She offered to take the day off and drive to Miami to pick me up there. It would have been significantly cheaper that way. I told my friend I appreciated the gesture, but didn't want her to go that far out of her way. The commuter flight was faster, anyway, since driving would have been at least six hours for Chevelle, round trip. More with traffic. I figure that springing for the extra flight is the kind of thing I might as well use the Callaway money for. Better than a carelessly run tour boat company, I suppose. But I digress.

Grandpa and Lottie need me. There's no time to waste.

When I finally arrive at my final destination, I collect my suitcase from baggage claim, then step out into the humid Florida heat and gaze at the sparkling blue water across the road from the airport. A pair of gulls fly overhead, cooing to each other as they bask in the sun. As if on cue, a dolphin jumps enthusiastically out of the water in the distance. Meanwhile, a turtle suns itself in a grassy area nearby. It feels like a welcoming committee somehow knows I'm back. It feels good.

It's remarkable how similar Hideaway Isle is as compared to my new home on Whidbey Island. So much alike are the stunning water views, the moisture in the air, and the distinctive plant and wildlife native to each island. Yet it's also entirely different. The juxtaposition is interesting to think about.

My concentration is broken by Chevelle's voice. She's rushing towards me with her arms outstretched, a huge smile on her face. She looks beautiful in an ombre rainbow maxi dress. It falls off her shoulder and has a tie around her trim waist. She has paired the dress with gold hoop earrings and coordinating nail polish. Her hair looks freshly dyed in a blonde hue. The curls bounce freely, just above her shoulders. My friend is flawless.

I feel underdressed in my jeans and gray Navy t-shirt. I reach up and smooth my hair back. It's tied in a ponytail, which is now askew after traveling overnight.

"Margot!" she practically screams as she grabs me and hugs me tightly. "It's so good to see you, my friend. And here on our very own Hideaway Isle, no less."

"Hey, Chev," I say as I hug her back. "I'll bet you never thought you'd live to see the day, eh?"

"You can say that again," she jokes. "Are you allergic to this place? Breaking out in hives yet? Throat closing shut?"

"Stop it," I say, chuckling. "You're so silly."

"Yeah, it's more fun that way," she replies. "The kids at school seem to appreciate my shenanigans. So many of them don't get enough fun at home. I do what I can to make up for that."

"You're the best," I say. "Those kids are lucky to have you. As am I. Keep the silliness going. I need all the comic relief I can get."

I suddenly notice a thirty-something guy who seems to be with Chevelle. He's hanging back, but he keeps glancing at us nervously. He looks nice enough. I wonder if he is Chevelle's boyfriend. She hadn't mentioned a boyfriend, but it seems possible. No ring on his finger. He's vaguely familiar. I don't think I know him, exactly, but I might have seen him around the island. I've been to so many places now that I sometimes imagine I recognize someone, only to realize later that they were in the wrong place to be the person I thought.

I lower my brows and shoot Chevelle a quizzical look to ask if this man is with her. She moves to follow my gaze.

"Oh, yeah," she says, turning towards him. "Puck, don't be shy. Come over here. Meet Margot."

He stumbles this way, nearly tripping over his own feet.

On second thought, if Chevelle is dating this man, I'll be surprised. She usually goes for the smooth and sophisticated type. Puck is definitely not that. He's a bundle of nerves.

"Um, hello," he says, shoving a hand in my direction. "Puck Reed. Nice to meet you."

"Margot Callaway," I say. "Nice to meet you, too."

I glance back at Chevelle, wondering why she brought this man to the airport. Maybe she's driving for a rideshare company in her spare time and he is a random passenger.

"Puck here wanted to meet you," Chevelle says. "He has something he wants to talk to you about."

"Oh, really?" I ask, confused as to what that something could be.

"Yeah," he confirms, sliding his hands into the pockets of his cargo shorts and shifting his weight nervously. "I'm sorry for the intrusion. I hope it isn't too much trouble."

I look at Chevelle for answers.

"You'll want to hear what he has to say," she assures me. "Do you have time for breakfast before you head to Grandpa Vern's?"

I open my smartphone to check the time, then look back at Chevelle.

It's awfully strange of her to put me in this position. I don't think she's ever done anything like this before. Maybe she's trying to set me up with Puck. Although that seems odd, too. He's too old for me. Chevelle knows my type as well as I know hers. I'm willing to date up to about four years older than me, but this guy is definitely beyond that. And while I don't mind a bit of charming dorkiness in a man, Puck appears far *too* dorky. Or maybe it's just his nervousness. Whatever it is, I'm not feeling a love connection. Surely, Chevelle knows that.

"We could eat at The Crumby Biscuit," she suggests.

She knows the locally owned diner is my old favorite breakfast joint. We used to go there before school on days when we could scrap together enough cash. They're a retro, hole-in-the-wall place that's oozing with character and Old Florida island charm. They don't try to compete with the fancier establishments, and their customers love them for it. You can show up at The Crumby Biscuit any time of day or night and get a tasty, hot meal in a casual atmosphere. Their bacon and egg biscuits are to die for. Not to mention, their french toast is heavenly. And their skillet fries are amazing. My mouth waters just thinking about it.

"Okay, sure," I say with a smile. "You had me at The Crumby Biscuit. How could I turn that down? But I can't stay long. My grandpa is waiting on me."

"I understand," Puck says. "I'm close to my grandpa, too. I won't keep you long. I promise."

"Alright then," Chevelle says, looping one arm through mine. "Knick Knack is this way."

Puck grabs my suitcase and carries it for me. I start to protest, but decide that I'm too tired to argue, so I let him carry it. It's a nice gesture.

"Knick Knack?" Puck asks.

"Mm hmm," Chevelle says as she struts. She's not showing off for Puck. She always walks like a show pony. "Knick Knack is what I call my little car," she continues. "She's so tiny, when I first saw her, I thought she should be on a shelf in my mama's curio cabinet. She's a pretty little thing though. Bright candy apple red with a spoiler on the back. Don't you worry. We'll all fit."

"Did you two ride here together?" I ask.

"No, we met near the terminal about fifteen minutes before you stepped out the door," Puck explains. "Although we've spoken on the phone several times."

"I see."

Good to know. So, they're not together. And it sounds like Chevelle doesn't know Puck well enough to try and set me up with him. Thank God. I'm not really in a good place for a new relationship at the moment. Certainly not with this guy.

"But we'll ride to the restaurant together?" I ask.

"Yeah, let's do," Chevelle says. "Nothing is far around

here. I'll drop Puck back at the airport once we get you settled."

Puck and I agree, then we pile into Chevelle's little red car and turn the air conditioning on full blast. It isn't even eight o'clock, but I can tell today is going to be a scorcher. Puck sits in the back next to my suitcase and I get comfortable in the passenger seat. I may not be interested in dating him, but I can tell he's trustworthy. I have no qualms about being with him like this, even though we've just met. He has a good-guy vibe about him. I'm at ease in his presence.

Chevelle lives walking distance from the elementary school where she works, so has suggested I share her car while I'm in town. I was planning to do so, but now that I see her shuttling Puck around like this, I decide to get a rental. I'll be here for a whole month. It makes sense to have my own vehicle available. I tell my friend about my change of plans. She puts up a bit of a fight, but finally agrees to take me to a rental car place after breakfast. I genuinely appreciate her willingness to help me out and make me feel welcome. I'm glad I have Chevelle in my life. I'm honestly not sure what I'd do without her.

The three of us chit chat on the short ride to The Crumby Biscuit, mostly about Washington State and how different it is. Chevelle says she'll come to visit me there soon. Puck tells me he's never been out of Florida, and that even within the state, he hasn't been further north than Orlando. I explain how I used to be the same way until I joined the Navy. Reflecting on the opportunities I've found for myself makes me feel proud. I left this place a naive kid. I'm returning as a confident, successful adult. And it's all my doing.

I get the impression that Puck is frustrated. I don't know anything about his life, but it seems like he longs for more. I'd like to learn about him. In a curious way, it seems like the two of us could be friends. Maybe I'll have a chance to see him more than once while I'm here, if he's interested in making a new friend.

6

THE WAY

We're seated at a booth in The Crumby Biscuit staring at thick paper menus by the time Chevelle finally starts the ball rolling. I'm sprawled out next to her, weary from the flights. Puck spreads himself widely on the bench across the table in similar fashion. I wonder what has made him weary. Sun streams in from a window beside us. Compared to Whidbey Island, it's as if someone turned a dial on the sun to max brightness. I'm not complaining. It's beautiful out.

We order a large spread of bacon, eggs, biscuits, and skillet fries, hungrily eyeing food as it passes us on its way to other tables. Once our waitress has gone to the kitchen to put our order in, we quiet down, ready to talk more seriously.

Not one to beat around the bush, Chevelle gets right to it.

"So, Margot," Chevelle says. "Puck contacted me in the hopes that I could get in touch with you on his behalf. Your trip here made for perfect timing."

I'm confused. "Why? And how?"

Puck looks nervous. He laces his fingers together and places his hands on the table in front of him.

"Where do I start?" he asks Chevelle.

She frowns, and I'm beginning to get the idea that whatever this is may be weightier than I realized.

"I'll try and set the stage," Chevelle says to Puck. Then she turns to face me in the booth.

"Is there a lot of stage to set?" I ask. "You two are kind of freaking me out."

They glance at each other.

"Wait," I say. "Is this about Lottie? And the boat tour company? Did... Oh, my God... Did you lose someone?"

My hand flies up to cover my mouth before I can stop it.

"No..." Puck says quickly. "I mean, it's sort of about Lottie, yes. And I lost someone, but not in the boat tour accident."

"Oh," I say, relieved. "Who did you lose?"

Puck takes a deep breath and I'm reminded of how Grandpa Vern and I have been doing the same.

"Most recently, I lost my grandmother," Puck says. "Mildred Finley."

"I'm sorry for your loss," I say.

"Thank you. She was killed in a lightning strike recently. It's terribly sad, but she had been diagnosed with Alzheimer's and was beginning to suffer. I have no doubt that she preferred to go in the strike. At least it was fast, and hopefully, not painful."

"I see," I reply. "I'm sure it's still sad. I've lost both of my parents. I know how hard it is to lose a loved one."

Puck wrinkles up his face like he might cry. Chevelle nudges me.

"You'll know his grandparents' house," she explains. "It's the big one on the water, just around the bend from the airport and Nimbus Marina. You know, wrap around porches. Big, pretty pool in the yard."

"Oh, right," I confirm. "I think I do know that house. So, you're from Hideaway Isle?"

"Yes," he says. "I wasn't sure about that until recently. You see, I couldn't remember anything from my early childhood."

I look at Chevelle, confused again. How could that be? Puck doesn't seem to have anything wrong with him that would have affected his development.

"Listen," she says.

"I... It's the strangest thing..." he continues. "I was struck by lightning as a kid. I was just five years old when it happened."

Chevelle nudges me again. "You remember hearing about that, right? A boy was hit while caught in a thunderstorm downtown and his parents didn't come to claim him. The Finleys took him in." She motions for Puck to continue.

"It wiped my memory clean," he explains. "I woke up in the hospital knowing very little. I could eat and walk and that kind of thing, but I couldn't remember identifying details about myself beyond my first name and my mother's first name. No guardians showed up for me. Like Chevelle said, the Finleys took me in."

"That story sounds familiar," I confirm. "Were you hurt? *Did* it hurt? The strike..."

"I don't remember much about the actual strike, but

yeah, I've had lingering effects. Headaches, nerve pain, anxiety, and my favorite-- depression."

"I'm so sorry," I say. "That sounds scary. I hate that it happened to you. Talk about being in the wrong place at the wrong time. What bad luck."

Puck seems touched. He pauses a moment, wiping a tear from his eye before he continues.

"Thank you," he says. "You're very kind. That means a lot to hear you say. I feel like you understand."

Chevelle smiles, like a facilitator who has successfully made a meaningful connection. Maybe she is, and maybe she has.

"But you said Mildred Finley was your grandmother, then Chevelle said the Finleys took you in... Was Mildred...? Was it actually your grandparents who took you in?" I ask, connecting the dots in my mind and hoping I'm not overstepping.

I'd feel terrible if I was nonchalantly glossing over details that are painful for Puck to talk about or hear. I know how upsetting it is to be on the receiving end of that treatment.

"Yes, exactly," he says. "And that's the craziest part of my story. I was actually struck by lightning at the same time as my grandmother a few weeks ago. She was holding onto a metal fence and I was trying to get her to come in from the storm. Anyway, I was struck for the second time in my life. When the bolt hit me, it somehow shook loose everything I hadn't been able to remember for all those years."

"Wow!" I say, genuinely amazed. "What a story. You should call The Today Show or something. They'd love to feature you. What are the odds?"

"I'm not interested in becoming any better known than I already am around here," he says. "I wish no one knew who I was, really."

"Oh, yes," I say. "I understand that, too. I don't know why I suggested it. I wouldn't want to be featured on The Today Show. I'm sorry I suggested it. I guess I'm not sure what to say. This is all very fascinating, but what does it have to do with me?"

Puck and Chevelle glance at each other again, then Puck looks down, avoiding eye contact with me.

"Go on, Puck, dear," Chevelle says. "Margot is a big girl. She can handle it."

I take Chevelle's hand under the table, sensing for certain now that this is big. I hope I can handle it. I'm glad she has faith in my ability to do so.

"Go ahead," I confirm.

"Okay," he says, taking another deep breath. "Margot, do you know your grandparents? I know you're here to see a Grandpa Vern, right?"

"Yes," I say. "My Grandma, Eloise, died before I was born."

"Vern and Eloise Callaway?"

"Vernon. But, yes."

He takes another deep breath. He finds the courage to meet my eyes, although I'm not sure what he's getting at.

"You lost your mom in an accident in Miami, right?" he asks reluctantly.

"That's right," I answer. "How did you know about that?"

"I found a newspaper article about it when I was

doing some research," he replies. "I'm sorry for your loss."

"Thank you," I say quickly, losing patience. I'm ready to hear what he's trying to say. "And?"

"Did you know her parents?"

I pause to consider the question. I didn't know Mom's parents. But I never received a solid explanation as to why not. She just said they were estranged. She was adamant that she didn't want Lottie and me to have any contact with them. I thought about looking for my maternal grandparents after Mom died, but I had no idea where to start. Mom never even told us her maiden name. She said it was too painful and would lead to nothing but heartache if we knew. I even asked Grandpa Vern about Mom's parents at one point. He claimed to not know any more than I did. Apparently, none of Mom's family came to the wedding when she married Dad. Chevelle knows these details. I debate whether or not to tell Puck.

"No," I say. "Unfortunately, I didn't. They were estranged. Why do you ask?"

Our waitress comes back with our food, but I don't feel like eating anymore. Puck seems to feel the same way. He disregards his breakfast plate as he focuses on me.

"I read that your mom's name was Annie," Puck says.

"Right, Annie Callaway," I confirm. "She was married to my dad, Jon Callaway. He was killed in a boating accident when I was a young child, in elementary school."

"I'm so sorry, Margot," Puck says. "You've had so much tragedy. So much loss."

"As have you," I say, oscillating between frustration and compassion for this poor man.

Puck looks at Chevelle for guidance. Her appetite hasn't been affected. She's slathering butter on a slice of french toast while chewing a strawberry.

"Change your approach," she mumbles, nodding at him.

Puck looks down, then out the window. I follow his lead, admiring the tropical landscaping outside. He collects his thoughts and begins again.

"I've been searching for my mom," he says. "Like I said, I didn't remember much until the second lightning strike that happened a few weeks ago. But now, I have vivid memories which were previously inaccessible to me. And I've spoken with my grandfather about what happened and what I remember. In fact, he was the one who told me he and Mildred were my grandparents. I had grown up thinking they were just adoptive parents. I wasn't aware of a genetic connection. I wish I had been."

My heart goes out to Puck. It must have been hard to learn a big secret like that. I imagine it's hard to trust when you know you've been lied to most of your life.

"Okay," I say, unsure of the best response.

"My grandfather, Herbert Finley, shared a letter with me that he's been holding for nearly thirty years. It was from my mother. His daughter. The combination of that letter and my newfound memories set me on the search to uncover more. I'm going to be a dad soon."

"Oh, wow," I reply. "Congratulations."

"Thanks," he says, smiling. "Yeah, my girlfriend, Chely, is pregnant. Knowing that I'll be a father makes me even more eager to understand my past. You know? I spent so many years in the dark. It... affected me... The not knowing..."

I nod, listening, frozen in place as I work to process how this relates to me. Chevelle continues to eat, slurping skillet fries and gulping orange juice. She's obviously heard all of this before. She keeps hold of my hand. I guess I can't be too upset with her. I just hope this story has a happy ending.

"I see," I manage.

Why does it feel like my life is about to be forever changed?

"Margot," Puck says, gaining strength. "My mom's name was Annie, too."

Oh, my God. I hold my breath, unable to breathe normally.

"Yeah?" I ask through clenched teeth.

"Margot, I know this will come as a shock," he says. "But I believe we have the same mother. I'm almost certain that your Annie Callaway is my Annie Reed. Which means that I'm your half-brother. Yours and Lottie's. And my grandparents, the Finleys, are your grandparents, too. Pop-- as I call him-- would love to meet you."

7

SOMETHING ELSE

I try to pick my jaw up off the floor as a sensation of burning from the inside out overtakes me. Adrenaline kicks in and I suddenly feel like a horse ready to rare up on my hind legs and kick anyone that gets too close.

"I have to go," I announce as I forcefully push Chevelle out of the way and stand. "Puck, it's been great," I say, reaching my hand out to shake his. "I'm afraid I can't stay here any longer."

I grab a twenty dollar bill out of my handbag and throw it down on the table to cover my breakfast. It's a shame. I was really looking forward to eating the food. There's no way I could keep anything down right now though. Maybe another day, if I last the entire month without hightailing it out of here. As of right now, I'd say the chances of that are fifty-fifty, at best.

"Where do you think you're going?" Chevelle asks as I make a beeline for the front door. "I have your suitcase, in Knick Knack..."

"I'll find you later," I say hastily as I make my way out

into what now feels like oppressive heat and sunlight. "I was getting a rental car anyway."

I let the door slam hard behind me. I walk briskly along the sidewalk in front of The Crumby Biscuit and don't slow down until I've passed five other establishments and am sure Chevelle and Puck aren't following. When I'm convinced it's clear, I squat near a bus bench and put my head between my legs. I think I might hyperventilate. *In and out*, I tell myself. *Slowly, in and out*. I'm conscious of my Navy t-shirt and how bad it must look to see a Naval Officer reduced to this. I can't help it. I don't think I could make myself stand and act put together if I had to. Thank God I'm not wearing my uniform.

This is exactly the kind of thing I was afraid of when I considered returning to Hideaway Isle. I couldn't articulate it, because I didn't know what was out there. I don't share Lottie's alleged psychic abilities. The best I have to work with is a scant few dreams about Mom. None seem particularly prophetic, or even otherworldly. They're just run of the mill dreams. I don't even dream about Dad. Yet something has seemed to be lurking here on this island, presumably waiting on me to come back so it could take me down again. And I can't be positive there isn't more than one thing lying in wait. I haven't seen Grandpa Vern or Lottie yet.

I'm practically shuddering, overwhelmed with emotion when a tall man with smooth, dark hair and a closely trimmed beard takes notice. He's carrying a bag of takeout from a Mexican restaurant behind me that apparently serves breakfast. At least, I think it's still breakfast time. Between the jet lag and my increasing levels of distress, I'm losing track.

He sees me, then slowly walks over as if he can't in good conscience leave someone this way. I guess I'd probably stop to help, too, if the roles were reversed. Any decent person would.

"Are you alright?" he asks, his voice deep and mellow.

I nod, too frazzled to speak. He glances around. I think he's checking to see if I'm with anyone. When he determines that I'm not, he walks over.

"Hey, there, Ms. Navy," he says. "You look like you could use a friend."

My face turns an even deeper shade of red at the mention of the Navy. I'm mortified. I do my best to say something intelligible, but I just don't have it in me. All I can manage is a sputter that sounds like an engine backfiring. The man looks around again, then squats beside me, setting his plastic takeout bag on the hot sidewalk.

His movements are slow and gentle. His breathing is calm. His presence is steady. I wonder if he's a doctor or similar. He seems to know how to deescalate a situation like a pro. I hate to be the one who needs talking down, yet here I am.

"I'll tell you a secret," he says softly. "I was in the Navy, too. No one around here knows about it."

My eyes widen. I don't know whether to be comforted or even more mortified, if that's possible. Now that I look at his face up close, I see that he is an exceptionally handsome man. He appears to be a few years older than me. No more than four. He must be at least a few inches taller than six feet, and he's in amazing shape. The muscles in his legs bulge as he balances himself on the balls of his feet.

"What was your MOS?" I ask.

That's short for military occupational specialty code. If he's former Navy, he'll know what the acronym means.

He smiles. "You really want to know?"

"Why not?" I ask, relaxing. He's like some kind of snake charmer, lulling me into a docile state.

"NOS E300."

"A frogman?"

"That's right," he confirms. "Did my six years and now I'm living the island life. How about you?"

He passed my test. He looks every bit the part of a Navy SEAL, too. Those guys can't disguise themselves, despite their best attempts. They are a certain type that trained eyes can recognize almost immediately. It took me a minute, but I see it clearly now.

I sit back onto the sidewalk, relieving the pressure on my knees. At this point, who cares if I'm seen sitting on the ground? I don't think my level of embarrassment can get any worse.

"NFO," I say, short for Naval Flight Officer. He'll know what it means.

"Ah," he replies, pleased. "A mustang?"

"Indeed. How could you tell?" I ask.

In the Navy, prior enlisted personnel who become officers are known as Mustangs. I enlisted and served before I enrolled in the Naval Academy, which means I fit the definition.

"You people have a look," he says with a chuckle. "What? Are you going to tell me you didn't guess I was a SEAL?"

"Touché," I say. "Although it took me a minute."

He shifts his weight, sitting down beside me. When he

stretches his long, muscular legs out in front of him, I feel my pulse quicken. There's something magnetic about this man. I was not expecting to meet someone like him today, that's for sure. I don't think I was *ever* expecting to meet someone like him. He seems like a rare breed.

"Rags Bertram," he says, reaching to shake my hand. "Former frogman hiding in plain sight. I own Nimbus Marina now, over near the airport."

"I know where the marina is," I say, taking his hand. It's warm. And strong. And huge. "I'm Margot Callaway. On leave from my squadron at Naval Air Station Whidbey Island."

He nods approvingly, then glances at my legs. I think he's checking me out. And if he is, well, let's just say I'd welcome his interest. I reach up and smooth my hair, disappointed to feel a slew of errant strands floating freely in the breeze. I hope he likes the disheveled type.

"Hey, you aren't related to Vern Callaway by chance, are you?" Rags asks.

"Actually, I am," I say, smiling now. "He's my grandpa. How do you know Vern?"

"Nice! Small world," Rags says. "He rents a slip at my marina."

"I didn't know he owned a boat," I reply. "Huh."

"He does. Such a stellar guy," Rags explains. "Your grandpa and I have become friends. We play golf together at least once a month. Out at his place. But he never told me he had a granddaughter in the Navy. A single, unmarried granddaughter in the Navy, right?"

I blush. I'm not sure how many additional shades of red my cheeks are capable of turning. It takes everything in me to keep from squealing like a schoolgirl right now. It really is incredible how life can turn on a dime. One of the worst days of my life may also turn out to be one of the best. Who would have thought?

Fate has a grip on me tightly. I'm not sure whether or not I wish to wriggle free. Maybe the bad is a package deal, necessary in order to get the good.

"Very single," I say, grinning. "Does Vern know you were in the Navy?"

"No. Like I said, it's a secret. For real. No one around here knows. I realize it's easy to spot a former SEAL if you know what you're looking for, but in general, I don't think the people around here do."

"Then I guess Vern wouldn't think it was relevant to mention me," I say.

Rags leans his incredibly strong shoulder against mine. "You know, you're spot on. What a coincidence though, me bumping into you like this. Am I right?"

His touch both electrifies and soothes me at the same time. It feels comfortable, like home. And not a wild, unpredictable home that's intent on upending you. More like a safe, stable home that's predictably kind and loving. I haven't had much experience with the latter, but I know it's what I want for myself going forward.

"Yeah, for sure," I say.

Rags takes his food out of the plastic container then opens a packet containing a miniature knife and fork. Without asking, he splits his breakfast burrito in two and hands me half. I take it and eat willingly. My appetite is back. Funny how that worked.

"Are you ready to tell me what you're doing out here, Margot?" he asks between bites. "Whatever it is, I'd like to help you with it."

I smirk. "Yeah, this looks bad," I say. "Promise you won't hold it against me?"

"Already purged from my mind," he jokes. "All except how pretty you look out here with the sunshine glistening on your darling face."

I practically spit out my bite of burrito. It's been a long time since I've been complimented like this. I'm giddy. The word darling makes me laugh though. I've never been good at the games people play while dating. I can't hold my genuine reactions back.

"What?" he asks, leaning his forehead towards mine.

"You said darling," I blurt. "What are you, from Alabama or something?"

He recoils in mock offense. "Hey, what if I am?" he asks. "Is that a deal breaker for the lovely Ms. Callaway of the honorable Naval Air Station Whidbey Island?"

"Nuh uh," I say. "Are you seriously from Alabama? Did I just insult you?"

We laugh together, and I realize that I'm completely at ease. Everything that had me in knots a short time ago has washed away thanks to Rags' calm demeanor. This man is like no other I've encountered. I swear. I'm here for it. He checks so many boxes on the list I've held in my head, reluctant to write down for fear I was asking too much in a man. And he's former Navy and friends with Grandpa Vern to boot. I can't wait to tell Chevelle.

"Not really Alabama," Rags says. "But close, sort of. South Carolina. And that's my real answer. I was born and raised in Mount Pleasant, a friendly little town outside of Charleston. Seriously, friendly. We've won awards and everything."

"Okay, then," I say, pursing my lips. "A true southern gentleman."

"Something like that," he replies. "So, Margot, I'll ask again. Do you want to tell me what has you out here like this today?"

I sigh. "Family stuff. I just received some shocking news, on top of having received other shocking news yesterday."

"Oh?" he asks, keeping his shoulder against mine. "Tell me about it?"

"It's a long story," I say. "I'm still trying to sift through the pieces and make sense of it all. I've been gone... I mean, I grew up here, but I haven't been back for seven years. My plane landed a few hours ago. I took a red eye from Seattle."

"Got it," he says, as if he understands.

I imagine he does understand. Rags shifts, bumping my shoulder again gently.

"What?" I ask.

"Can I take you somewhere?" he offers. "I know we just met, but Vern can vouch for me. I promise I'm not a weirdo stalker or anything. Maybe then we'll have time to talk some more. It sounds like you have a lot to get off your chest."

I consider his proposal. If he knows Vern, I'm sure it's fine. I'm a pretty good judge of character, anyway, and I have zero concerns about this guy. In fact, I want to spend more time with him. The feeling is different than I've experienced before.

"That would be nice," I say. "I need to rent a car. Can you take me to a rental place? I was going to share my friend Chevelle's while I'm in town, but I don't want to put her out."

He nods. "I can do you one better. You can borrow my Sequoia."

"Oh, I…" I begin.

"It's fine. Really," he interjects. "I keep it for the cargo space, but I'm more of a Jeep guy at heart. I have a Wrangler that I'll drive while you're using the Sequoia."

He sounds sure.

"I don't know," I say. "We just met… Me huddling near a bench like some kind of crazy person. Besides, I wouldn't want to inconvenience your wife… or girlfriend… or whatever…"

He laughs heartily now, leaning back and placing a hand on top of his taut abs, his head tilted at a happy angle.

"Was that your attempt at asking if I'm single?" he replies. "Because I am. How did you say it? *Very* single."

I laugh, too. "I have no game," I admit bashfully.

"You don't need game with me," he says, his tone becoming thoughtful. "I'm a straight shooter. I tell it like it is. What you see is what you get… All of that…"

I squint and place one hand above my eyes to block the sun, sizing him up.

"Okay, Rags," I say, his name feeling good in my mouth. "I'd appreciate you letting me borrow your Sequoia, if you're sure it isn't any trouble."

"None at all."

"And I'd like to see you again," I say, proud of my bravery.

This guy is something else. I don't want to screw around and pass up the chance to get to know him better.

"I'd like that, too," he says.

We hold eye contact, smiling at each other.

"How about right now?" he asks. "Where are you going next? Maybe I can tag along."

"Don't you have other things to do?" I ask. "Work?"

I protest, but in reality, I'd love nothing more than to spend time with him right now. And forever.

Stop it, I tell myself. *Slow down.*

"I did have work," he replies. "But since I own the business, I can exercise the option to blow work off and instead get to know the most beautiful, intelligent, and magnetic woman I believe I've ever met. Especially since she'll only be in town for a few short weeks. The clock's ticking. I don't want to miss a thing."

I practically melt right into the ground below me. I think I'm smitten. I've never believed in love at first sight. Now, I don't know. What I do know is that I have things to tend to. Difficult, dramatic, and life altering things. I could use a friend.

"Noted," I say. "So, I had planned to head to Vern's condo next. You know, once I was finished crouching by this bench. Want to join me for a visit?"

"You had me the moment I laid eyes on you in your badass Navy t-shirt, Margot Callaway. We've all spent time crouching by benches, whether real or metaphorical. I'm just glad I was here in this place and time to sit with you while you crouched by yours today."

I lean against his shoulder, a subtle embrace. I hope it's the first of many.

"To Vern's?" I ask. "We can swing by and get the Sequoia after."

"To Vern's," Rags replies. "I know the way."

8

LOOSEN

"Little M!" Grandpa Vern shouts as he bursts out the front door of his condo to embrace me.

I hug him tightly, happy to feel his warm cheek against mine.

Grandpa looks good. Healthy. He picks me up and twirls me around, barely noticing Rags. I'm surprised by his spunk. The lines around Grandpa Vern's eyes are deeper and I think he might be balder, if that's possible considering his near total baldness before. Otherwise, he looks just the same as the last time I saw him. He's spry for his age. I'll bet he has to beat the ladies off with a stick.

"It's good to see you, Grandpa," I say.

"Come in. Where are your things? You are planning to stay with me, aren't you?"

His voice trails off as he asks, like a kid who has been disappointed one too many times and so doesn't allow himself to get excited anymore. It hurts to hear. I was planning to stay with Grandpa, but after the morning I just had, I need some peace and solitude. I hope it doesn't hurt his feelings too badly.

"My suitcase is in Chevelle's car," I explain. "I think I'm going to get a hotel room, Grandpa. No offense. I'm used to living alone. I like my space."

"Okay," he says. "No offense taken."

"I promise I'll be over here a lot. You'll want rid of me by the time I go back to Washington."

"Never," he says with a smile.

Finally, he notices Rags. "Hey, there, Rags, my friend," Grandpa says. "I can't golf today. My granddaughter here is in town. This is Margot."

"We've met," Rags says in what I've now come to believe is the sexiest voice I've ever heard. It makes the hair on the back of my neck stand up, in a good way.

I might have other motivations for wanting my own hotel room. This is my life. As tempting as it is to revert back to feeling like a child while in Hideaway Isle, I'm an independent adult. I choose to act like one. If Rags pays me a visit to hang out in private, so be it.

"Oh? Did you two pull in at the same time? What luck, eh?" Grandpa asks.

Apparently, Grandpa hasn't considered Rags and me as a potential couple. If he had, he would have mentioned it. He talks about eligible bachelors from time to time during our phone conversations. I wonder why he overlooked this fine hunk of man right here in front of his face.

"Not exactly," I say, smiling up at Rags.

"We met at breakfast," he offers, an adorable smile on his adorable face.

Rags doesn't mention the fact that breakfast was eaten

out of a takeout container while sitting on a sidewalk. I kind of like how we have inside jokes and stories already. If, by some miracle, we should end up together, today's breakfast will be a story we tell our grandchildren. I like the thought of that.

"Marvelous," Grandpa Vern says. "How did you figure out that I knew the both of you?"

Rags and I glance at each other, and all at once, Grandpa catches on to the connection between us. Recognition washes over his face. He was young and in love back in the day. He knows what attraction looks like.

"When I introduced myself," I say. "I told him my last name…"

"And I asked if she was related to you," Rags says, finishing my sentence.

Grandpa Vern smiles the biggest smile, like a proud papa. Apparently, he approves. I'm so glad. We might be onto something here.

We're still standing in the open-air breezeway outside of his condo. Tropical birds call to each other insistently in the distance. I'd forgotten how loud they can be. I'm beginning to break a sweat. I'm no longer used to the climate.

"Are you going to invite us in?" I ask with a smile.

"Yes!" Grandpa says, slapping a hand to his forehead for dramatic effect. "Sorry! I don't know where my mind is today. Come in."

He turns and gestures for us to follow him inside. From the looks of it, the condo is just as it was the last time I saw it, too. The rattan bar stools sit dutifully next to the counter. The pull-out sofa lines the edge of the living room wall, the same pillows in tropical palm print placed neatly on top. The coffee and end tables are the same glass tops supported by bamboo frames. The view of the water is still stunning. I don't immediately notice traces of Lottie having spent the better part of six years here.

Rags makes conversation while I assess the place. He seems comfortable being here. Apparently, he's been here plenty of times before.

"From what Margot tells me," he begins, speaking to Vern, "the two of you have a lot on your plate."

"Indeed, we do," Grandpa confirms. "Too much, if you ask me. I'm just glad Margot came back to help out. I don't know if I could get through this without her. Her sister..."

Rags nods slowly. "If it's alright with you, Vern," he says, "I'd like to stick around and help. I have the time, and it seems like Margot could use the support. We sort of hit it off right away."

Grandpa and Rags both glance at me, waiting for a reaction.

"Did we?" I ask, joking, as I trace a finger along a row of family photos that have been framed and hung on the wall.

"Oh, don't be shy, Little M," Grandpa says. "Let it happen."

Rags smiles at us both, satisfied, then sits down in a bamboo rocker and puts his feet up on the coordinating ottoman. He moves back and forth smoothly. I pause, trying my best to kid around by making a pouty face, but my own smile forces its way through. I plop down on the sofa beside Grandpa Vern, relaxed and ready to face what awaits me. It all seems more manageable with Rags around. For the first time in a long time, I feel like I'm doing what I should be in life, at the right place at the right time. I'm here with Grandpa, helping him out with Lottie. I'm in the flow, rather than against it.

"Fine," I say. "I'll let it happen."

"Good," Rags says emphatically. "Let it happen."

"Yeah, good," Grandpa echoes. "Rags is a good guy, Margot. I'd trust him with my life."

"Wow," Rags says. "I didn't realize that, Vern, but the feeling is mutual."

The two men bond over their shared admiration of each other. Meanwhile, I nod and move my eyebrows up and down a couple of times. It feels silly, but it matches my mood. I feel lighter, and strangely, better equipped to do what I must.

"Okay, then. Shall we get started?" I ask. "Because I have to tell you what happened to me this morning, Grandpa. *Before* I met Rags."

"I guess," Grandpa says. "But I need to tell you what happened to *me* this morning. Things have... progressed... since I spoke to you on the phone yesterday."

"This is something different," I explain. "It's not about Lottie. At least, not directly. And not just about Lottie. It concerns Mom."

I'm not sure how Grandpa Vern will take the news about Puck. If Puck turns out to be a half-brother to Lottie and me, it doesn't really affect Grandpa. His relationship to Mom was that of a father-in-law. If she had another child before she met Dad, what would Grandpa Vern care? Grandpa might be very happy to see his granddaughters welcomed into another family. He wants the best for us. I know that for sure. It does seem weird to think of Mom having a child before me though. If she had a child that she somehow abandoned, that's another story. I'm not sure how any of us could think of her the same if we found out that was the case. I know I'd be disappointed.

Rags looks at me curiously. He folds his muscular arms over each other, then waits quietly to hear what I have to say. He seems to be cataloguing my family history as he learns it. I appreciate his efforts. I make a mental note to ask about his family the first chance I have. I doubt they're as messed up as mine. I hope I don't scare him off.

"Okay, interesting," Grandpa says. "It just seems like we can catch up on other things later. What I have to tell you is urgent. Can I please go first?"

Rags shrugs. He's not going to weigh in since he's new here, but he seems to believe Grandpa and I have plenty of time to say everything we need to. I get the idea Rags is a mellow type that never gets too worked up. I guess you sort of have to be that way to be a good SEAL. Although I've met other SEALs who are higher strung. At any rate, I like his low-key attitude. I think his temperament would make a good complement to my own.

"Sure," I say. "What I have to tell you is so out of left field, anyway. I guess it isn't directly related to the situation with Lottie."

"Thank you," Grandpa replies. "We'll get through it all. I promise."

I catch Rags up, explaining Mom's accident, Grandpa Vern's money, my disappearing act and life in the Navy, and Lottie's recent troubles. Periodically, I glance at Grandpa to make sure he's okay with me sharing all of this information. He is. It feels cathartic to get it all out in the open. Something about telling my story to Rags and in front of Grandpa at the same time provides me tremendous relief. It feels like a new beginning. I know I have a tough road ahead of me as we work to right Lottie's path, but I truly think we'll find a way to do it. We have to. We've come too far now to give up. I'm back on Hideaway Isle, after all. When I'm done with the lengthy explanation, Grandpa scoots forward in his seat, ready to tell us what happened this morning.

"It was a knock at my door," he begins. "And a phone call, at the same time. It sent a chill down my spine. I'm not a superstitious person, but it struck me the wrong way. Like I could feel evil lurking nearby."

"Really?" I ask.

This doesn't sound like Grandpa Vern at all. He's really spooked.

"Who was it?" Rags asks.

"That's the thing," Grandpa continues. "I answered the phone first, thinking it might be Margot. She had told me her flight information, so I knew it was too early for her to be at the door. Someone was on the line because there wasn't a dial tone. But they didn't respond when I said hello."

"How early was it?" I ask.

"Not long after six. I was awake, but I'm not sure I've ever gotten a call that early, let alone a knock on the door at the same time. Usually, I'm awake by five thirty, all by myself. Just me and the birds and the dolphins."

"And was anyone at the door?" Rags asks.

"It took me a few minutes to get to it since I was troubling with the phone," Grandpa explains. "But no. No one was there. I went out into the breezeway to look around. I even went downstairs to the ground level. I didn't see anyone. Nothing out of the ordinary. It was bizarre."

Rags nods. "What do you make of it, Vern?"

Grandpa wrings his hands and shrugs his shoulders. "I don't know what to make of it."

"But you mentioned evil lurking?" I ask. "What makes you think so?"

"A gut feeling," he replies. "I remember when I was a kid, my parents would tell stories of organized crime up north and how the mob bosses had ways of sending you a message if they wanted to make you cooperate."

"That's where your mind is?" Rags asks.

I study Grandpa Vern and can't help but notice how frail he is. Just because he looks nearly the same as the last time I saw him and is in great shape for his age doesn't mean he is strong enough to hold his own in a physical altercation. If someone were to rough him up, he'd be at their mercy. Vern is a sweet, gentle man. He wouldn't hurt a fly. It would be heartbreaking to see him in trouble through no fault of his own.

I lean towards my grandpa and place a hand on his forearm. Rags nods and winks at me, as if he knows what I'm going to say.

"Grandpa Vern," I say. "Do you have a weapon here? For... protection?"

9

BREACH

R ags and I are in the kitchen of Grandpa Vern's condo, gathering tea and toast for a mid-morning snack when we hear a forceful knock on the front door. Grandpa is in the living room, closest. I glance through the narrow opening between rooms to see how he will react. I'm not sure how often Grandpa gets visitors. Maybe it's someone benign, like a neighbor asking to borrow a cup of sugar or wondering if he wants to play a round of golf. Yet what if it's not? What if it's someone more nefarious? I glance at Rags, who is alert. He follows my gaze into the living room.

Grandpa stands hesitantly, then walks to the closed door and looks through the peephole to see who is there. My muscles tense. Maybe it's because Grandpa Vern was just talking about evil lurking and such, but I'm on edge. I fear that the trouble Lottie is in might find its way to our vulnerable grandpa. It's hard to predict what might happen, especially since I am nowhere near up to speed on what my sister has gotten herself into. But people died, apparently due to Lottie's negligence. That's bound to stir up trouble. Thank God Rags and I are here with Grandpa now. I hate to think it, but I suspect he may need us.

I can hardly believe that just twenty-four hours ago, I was at my desk on Whidbey Island, wearing my Navy uniform, gazing out at the Puget Sound while thinking about whale watching, and generally going about my business as usual. Grandpa hadn't called. I hadn't spoken with Chevelle. I didn't know Lottie was in trouble. Or that she claimed to have psychic powers. In my naivety, I thought any threat serious enough to turn my world upside down would come as part of my service to my country in the military. Within that framework, I knew I could be called to respond on short notice if my squadron was needed. Every active duty service member knows that. I never dreamed that I'd be called back to Hideaway Isle, or that I'd get involved in the strange unfolding of my sister's liability and consequences come home to roost.

As Grandpa unfastens the deadbolt and begins to turn the knob, I move to follow him. I want whoever is there to know he isn't alone. Rags reaches out an arm, stopping me. I look at him, confused. I'm tempted to fling his arm away and walk into the living room with my grandpa. After all, Rags and I just met. I don't owe him any allegiance. Grandpa Vern's safety is my priority. But I pause.

Rags' background as a Navy SEAL means he is highly trained for this exact type of situation. If whoever is at the door has bad intentions, Rags' training is our biggest asset. The Navy trained me in basic self-defense and I've taken some Jiu Jitsu classes for fun, but I never expected to find myself in a situation where I'd need anything more. Rags, on the other hand, is skilled as a literal killing machine. I don't have to ask what he knows. By virtue of his experience as a Navy SEAL, I can be certain of his competence. I'm sure his instincts are sound. I decide to follow his direction.

Rags places a finger over his lips, telling me to be quiet. I nod my understanding. He wraps his arm around me, pushing me behind him and against a row of kitchen cabinets. His eyes are fixed on the space between rooms and his body is angled in what appears to be a strategic position. I follow his line of sight and realize that he's watching the reflection on one of the glass doors leading out to the lanai. In the reflection, he has an unobstructed view of the front door area that we wouldn't otherwise be able to see from our position.

He looks back at me, then raises his hands in the air to let me know that his actions are methodical. I nod again. My heart races, but there's no time to falter. I'm ready to do my part. Slowly, Rags pulls a handgun out of a holster on the inside of his belt, careful not to make a sound. It looks like a Glock. Probably the same kind he used in the military. No doubt, Rags is comfortable with the weapon and highly attuned to its intricacies. He looks at me again, hard, to make sure I'm okay with this. We communicate with our facial expressions and strategic gestures. I nod again, more slowly this time, with my eyes narrowed and my shoulders back. He seems to want to know if I have a weapon on me. I don't, although now I wish I did. I own a handgun. I left it at my apartment on Whidbey Island because I didn't want to go through the hassle of flying with it. I hate that I left it behind. Gathering my resolve, I raise my hands and shake my head to indicate that I'm unarmed. Rags motions for me to stay back, his smooth black hair shifting on his head and gleaming under the fluorescent ceiling lights. He intends to handle this alone.

In a split second, as I take in the scene unfolding around me, I think Rags might be overreacting. Grandpa Vern's kitchen counter is cluttered with orange rinds from the freshly squeezed juice he made this morning, along with various items Rags and I were working on. It all looks so domestic and innocuous. It looks typical for a retiree living in a condo in South Florida who just welcomed mid-morning guests. I'm sure there are thousands of other kitchens in condos much like this one with very similar contents splayed about. How do we go from orange rinds, toast, and tea to a raised gun? It's dizzying, to say the least. Not to mention, I didn't know Rags had a concealed carry. I guess I shouldn't be surprised. And I'm *not* surprised if I stop to think about it. I just wasn't focused on that kind of thing in this setting. Rags is dressed in olive shorts and a button down, collared shirt with palm leaf print. He seemed so laid back. The swift change of pace is a little jarring.

Rags senses my bewilderment. He's trained to move past that. He knows not to hesitate. Glancing quickly between me and the reflection of the front door, he grabs one of my hands and gives it a quick squeeze. It seems to say that I should trust him. And I do. I shake my head, hoping to shake off any doubt.

Grandpa Vern opens the front door.

"Good morning, gentleman," he says, and I can tell his voice is strained.

I'm not sure whether the guys at the door detect Grandpa's thinly veiled distress. Rags waits, gun steady, eyes peeled. I'm ready, too, although I don't know exactly what I'll do if this goes sideways and my help is needed. I really wish I'd brought my gun.

I hear a few minutes of murmuring from the guys at the door, then Grandpa Vern's voice again. It sounds solid this time. Resigned.

"Do what you want with me. But please, don't hurt her," he says.

To my horror, a single gunshot rings out. It makes a heavy thump. The sound instantly sickens me and I have to cover my mouth so I don't throw up. I know from my training that the bullet has most likely hit something soft and dense, like the sofa, maybe. Or a human body. All of a sudden, my perception becomes a distorted whirr of sights and sounds, much like the day Mom died. I recognize the terror. The sensation of falling down while standing up. The ringing in my ears that won't let me think straight, let alone take measured action. I'm frozen. Helpless, as I choke back vomit and flail around, grasping for something substantial to hold onto. Or so it seems.

Without a moment's hesitation, Rags bursts into the living room, his gun drawn. I watch him through the space between rooms, then through the reflection in the glass door. He moves strategically, keeping his center of gravity low and his awareness acute. His muscular body is prepared for anything. He moves towards the door.

"Put your hands up where I can see them," Rags shouts. "Right now. Hands up or I'll shoot."

I see shapes and shadows moving in the breezeway, then loud voices. Men's voices. I don't see Grandpa. My heart pounds so hard it seems it might beat right out of my chest. The shapes in the breezeway disappear, then I hear loud footsteps clamoring down the stairs.

"They're getting away," I say to Rags in a low voice that doesn't even sound like my own.

I feel distant from myself. I'm detached. And frightened. I don't know what to do. As if on cue, Rags turns and tells me.

"I'm going after them," he says. "Lock this door behind me and call 9-1-1." Then, when I don't respond, "Margot, do you hear me? I need you to focus."

I close my eyes, wishing I could be anywhere but here. I don't hear my grandpa's voice. I don't see him moving around in the reflection. Tears sting at my eyes as I try to comprehend what has taken place. I want to cover my ears like a little child would do. To cover my eyes. To hide my head like an ostrich in the sand. The strange animal suddenly seems completely relatable.

"Margot," Rags says. "You can do this. You've been trained for the unexpected. I'm counting on you, okay? Lock this door and call the police. Don't let anyone but officers with a badge in until I get back. Okay?"

I force myself to function, nodding and moving forward. "Okay," I reply.

I walk into the living room in time to watch Rags burst out the front door, stepping over Grandpa Vern along the way.

"Oh, my God," I say out loud. My voice seems like it's coming from someone else.

Grandpa is on his back on the living room floor, a

small gunshot wound in the middle of his forehead. His eyes are open, but they're vacant. It doesn't seem like he's here with me anymore. Blood drips from the back of his head onto the smooth tan tile below.

I stare at the open front door in shock, struggling to believe that any of this is real. I'm not sure how long I stay in the same spot, frozen, until I finally do as Rags said and I shut and lock the door. Mustering all of my strength, I go to Grandpa Vern's landline phone on the wall and I dial 9-1-1. I'm not sure why I choose the landline instead of calling from my mobile phone, but it seems like the right thing to do. The operator will probably be able to find Grandpa's address faster this way, and time is of the essence.

"9-1-1, what's your emergency?" the soft female voice on the other end of the phone says.

"Yes, um…" I begin, my voice failing me. "I…"

"Ma'am, do you have an emergency?"

"Yes," I reply. "My grandpa has been shot. I… I don't know what to do…"

She says something in the background. Or maybe it isn't in the background. I can't tell.

"Okay, help is on the way. Is he breathing?"

"How do you know the address?" I ask, practically unaware that I had just considered the address lookup when I picked up and dialed this phone moments ago.

"We have the address," the woman says. "Ma'am, your grandpa. Is he breathing?"

I turn back to look at Grandpa Vern. He's gone. I know he is. He's been gone since we heard the gunshot. His body is still, seized by senseless violence, his life cut short and taken against his will. My heart doesn't want it to be true, but my mind knows it is. He was killed execution style in his own condo by mystery men who don't care who they hurt. And Rags is chasing after those men somewhere, some way. If they shot Grandpa like this in cold blood, they won't hesitate to shoot Rags, too. He's in grave danger. I'm speechless.

"I don't…" I stammer. "No. I don't think so. There's a gunshot wound to his head. He's… bleeding out on the tile floor. There's a lot of blood. I think he's… gone."

PART II

PHENOMENON

10

PURSUITS

I remember a time when my family was intact, whole and healthy: Mom, Dad, Grandpa Vern, Lottie, and me. It only lasted for a few short years between the time Lottie was born and Dad died, but at least I know what whole and healthy is. Some people never get a single day of what I had during those years. I'm acutely aware of how lucky that makes me. I think about it from time to time, when I'm lying awake at night, unable to sleep. Just because I've stayed away from Hideaway Isle doesn't mean I'm not grateful. And now, hearing Puck's story then seeing another beloved family member killed, I realize how truly precious that era was.

I was a precocious third grader when most of my happiest memories took place. It was a year of wonder. Mom and Dad were content with their lives and each other, Lottie was a cheerful baby, and Grandpa Vern was the perfect doting grandfather. Our days were filled with family gatherings around the dinner table, evening walks on the beach, and weekend adventures, often taking place in the sparkling waters around our little island.

We lived right on the water then, in a little yellow house facing Kestrel Cay, on the west side of the island. Life was surely grand. I remember the wide swing on our back porch and the haute blue paint on the ceiling, the potted hydrangeas on the patio, and the pair of kayaks we kept hanging from the roof of the garage, ready to load onto the minivan at a moment's notice for an impromptu trip. Our house wasn't anything fancy, but Mom kept it orderly and welcoming. My friends from school used to beg their parents to let them spend the night. Maybe it was because they wanted to play with my baby sister, but I think Mom's freshly baked cookies and warm smiles had a little something to do with it, too. Mom didn't work then. Dad's job at the local bank afforded her the luxury of being a stay-at-home mom. I'm sure glad it did. Life was easy in a relaxed, wholesome way. If I ever get married and have kids, I want my children to feel the same sense of belonging and effortless acceptance. I want them to know what it is to be thoroughly loved. Every human should know what that's like. I count my lucky stars that I do.

It was that year when I fell in love with reading, spurred by Dad's passion for stories and the magic they can create. I began with Beverly Cleary's Amelia Bedelia, Ramona Quimby, and Ralph S. Mouse, which were written specifically for kids my age. I remember dragging those books along with me everywhere I went, pages dog eared and notes scribbled in the margins. I couldn't get enough. To this day, I almost always have a novel in my hands or loaded on my e-reader. As an adult, I'm a huge thriller fan, thanks to Dad. He loved Tom Clancy and even though I was too young for that level of intensity at the time, the sight of my dad with the latest Jack Ryan novel in his hands stands out in my mind. As soon as I was old enough, I checked Clancy's novels out for myself. Reading them helped me feel connected to Dad. It might sound silly, but when you've lost a parent, you do what you can to keep from feeling lost and alone in the world. When you've lost both parents, much of your waking awareness is an effort to keep from feeling lost and alone in the world. I've done my best.

It was also during my year of wonder when I came to appreciate wildlife and our responsibility to protect it. I distinctly remember Dad taking me to the beach one August evening to watch as baby sea turtles hatched from their eggs and made the perilous crawl to the big, dangerous sea. I remember thinking how brave they were. Their chances of survival were slim, yet they courageously forged on anyway. I suppose Lottie and I did the same thing, if you think about it. I didn't know it at the time, but our future would involve much the same level of risk against terrible odds. Yet we press forward, into the unknown, handling some obstacles better than others.

If I knew then what I do now, I'd probably be too overwhelmed to continue. I imagine I'd resign myself to a life of trepidation and drudgery, much like Lottie apparently has. I sometimes wonder how I came through the trauma I've faced so well. Is it my nature that makes me more resilient than Lottie? Am I inherently better able to cope? Or is it nurture? Did those extra seven years with Mom and Dad afford me a jump on personal development that Lottie can never catch up on by virtue of her moment of birth? What a cruel world it is to rob one child of the opportunities another from the same family is afforded. The premise makes me feel terribly guilty, but also thankful. I suppose I'll need to be strong enough for the both of us.

As I sit on Grandpa Vern's sofa waiting for the emergency medics, his lifeless body on the floor nearby, I know that I must pick up the phone and call my sister. Her already fragile world is about to be shattered into a million more pieces. Even so, she needs to hear this from me. I'm the only older relative she has now. I don't count Puck and his grandpa because I don't have the mental bandwidth to deal with that right now. Or anytime soon, for that matter. Even if they do turn out to be related to us, Lottie and I don't have a history with them. It's different. Lottie will need me, whether the two of us like it or not. We will need each other. I have to tell her what happened to Grandpa Vern. And I have to warn her. The guys who shot Grandpa may be after Lottie. It's too soon to tell for sure, but it's likely that my sister is in danger. I won't lose her, too. I can't.

I stand, stepping around Grandpa's body, and walk to the bar where his landline phone is located. I feel the urge to stop and embrace Grandpa's body along the way. I'd like to give him one last kiss on the cheek or lean my head on his warm chest one more time before it cools forever, but I don't. I need to reach Lottie. Every moment is precious. Hopefully, if she sees the caller ID as Grandpa Vern's, she'll answer. I'm not sure she'd pick up if she knew it was me, and I really don't want her hearing this news from a stranger.

I slide onto a rattan stool, just like I imagine Grandpa Vern did all those times we talked on the phone when I was living away these past seven years. It saddens me now to consider how much I missed. Maybe I'll feel better when I'm further away from the fresh trauma of my current situation, but I'm wishing I'd never enlisted in the military. Grandpa Vern was nothing but patient and kind to me. He deserved better than a granddaughter who was too selfish to come home and take care of her family. I could kick myself. I'm so ashamed. I feel like I've dishonored the people who mean the most. I feel like such a fool.

I wipe my eyes, pushing the emotion back in favor of tending to the task at hand. There will be plenty of time for reflection later. Referencing Grandpa Vern's list of names and numbers recorded in his distinctive handwriting with a ballpoint pen and taped to a wall next to the phone, I pick up the receiver and dial my sister's number. Each number feels laborious as I choose it. Dialing Lottie to tell her this terrible news is perhaps the hardest thing I've ever done. It's harder than seeing Mom's accident or Grandpa Vern's. Probably because I'm the only person Lottie has left to look up to. I don't want to see her hurt. It breaks my heart. I want to somehow buffer and protect her from the dreadfulness in this world. I want to make things better for her, not worse. I hate feeling this helpless to cushion her blow. It's agony.

"Hey, Grandpa," she says after a few rings.

It's her. Her voice is all grown up now, deeper and fuller. But I recognize it. Much like I felt when I first saw my sister's picture earlier this morning, she may have grown and changed, but I recognize her essence as the same.

I hesitate. Once I speak and she knows it's me, Lottie may recoil and disappear. I'm struck by the possibilities that hang in the balance. We're at a crossroads, my sister and I. Our lives could take radically different directions from this point forward. So much depends on whether the two of us come together or grow further apart.

"Lottie, it's me," I say, softly but firmly.

I don't want to sound weak. I need to inspire confidence. She's quiet on the other end of the line.

"It's Margot."

No response.

"Your sister."

The line goes completely silent, then I hear a dial tone. *Damn.* I dial again. She picks up, but she blasts me.

"Margot! Damn you!" she shouts. "You have some nerve calling me after all these years. You may have wormed your way back into Grandpa Vern's life, but I'm not so easily fooled…"

"Lottie," I say calmly. "I have something serious to tell you. I mean it."

"Yeah? You don't have shit to say to me for seven whole years, and now you want to talk to me about something serious? Bullshit, Margot. You are full to the brim with bullshit. Stay out of my life."

I hear a click and she's gone again. I take a deep breath, then dial her a third time. I hear the call connect, but she doesn't say anything.

"Lottie, please don't hang up," I say. I hear my detached tone. I'm not sure what other tone to strike, or how to pull it off. "This is important. Are you sitting down?"

As I ask, I suddenly realize that I don't even know where my sister lives. Grandpa said she moved out last year, but I have no idea how to find her. If I scare her off, I won't know where to begin with a search. Maybe Rags can help. Or Chevelle. If Rags is okay, that is. And Chevelle, well, maybe I shouldn't get her involved in this. *Shit.*

"What?" Lottie snaps, her voice like that of a feral animal that's been cornered against its will.

"I didn't want you to hear this news from a stranger," I explain. "I'm at Grandpa Vern's condo… and…"

Lottie screams in frustration. It sounds like a roar. She's so vocal. So dramatic. I guess I didn't expect that. I'm much more low-key and soft spoken by comparison. Lottie sounds like someone has just ripped a bandaid off of her, and she's a tender, raging ball of energy.

"I'm sorry," I say.

I'm apologizing for more than I can articulate. I'm sorry she's upset. I'm sorry about the bad news I have to deliver. I'm sorry she got the short end of the stick in our family. And I'm sorry I left her. How can I adequately express any of these things?

"Margot," my sister says through gritted teeth, "You had better spit whatever this is out. I'm losing patience with you. You have three seconds and then I'm hanging up for good. Three…"

"Lottie, come on," I say. "This isn't a time for games. I have…"

"Two…"

"Lottie!" I shout, meeting her mood.

"One…"

"Dammit, Lottie. Grandpa Vern has been killed," I blurt, exasperated. "Shot in the head just now when he answered a knock on his front door. The shooters took off. First responders are on their way. We're in danger."

I don't mention Rags. Or Puck. Or the fact that I know about the tour boat company and the accident. There isn't time. Lottie and I simply *must* get together and talk. Really talk, for the very first time in our lives.

11

SUPPOSITION

I'm still on the stool with the phone to my ear when I notice a trio of young paramedics rushing in from the parking lot and heading my way. I can see them-- all male-- from the screens over the lanai. They're practically running, a stretcher balanced between two of them and a large red medical bag with a white cross on it carried by the third. They're all wearing the same black pants and crisp white uniform shirts. I appreciate their urgency, even though they're too late to help Grandpa. If he was clinging to even a thread of life, I'd jump up and usher them in. He's not. His body is chillingly still, his eyes fixed on something he must have seen at the moment of his death. I remain seated and watch, overwhelmed by my present circumstances.

There's something comforting about people in uniform, except when they're coming towards you. Then the gravity of it all hits like a ton of bricks. These men will take Grandpa Vern out of this condo for the last time. He'll leave like he has countless times, but he won't return. Ever. The permanence is unsettling.

"Lottie?" I say into the telephone.

It's too late. My sister has disconnected the call. I don't know where to find her beyond dialing the same number again. I doubt she'd answer. I suppose I'll have to wait for her to find me. *I can do that*, I think. I just need to stay put. I probably can't handle much more anyway. I slam down the receiver, my hands unsteady.

I'm not sure what I'm supposed to be doing right now. I guess I should simply wait. Move through it. One foot in front of the other, when it's time. The sights and sounds around me seem strangely foreign. Words and letters swim around in my mind and then separate, out of order like alphabet soup. Maybe it's the exhaustion and the stress. In many ways, this takes me right back to the day Mom was killed. Memories of the adrenaline coursing through me, the way my body seems to be sending mixed signals as if it could short circuit, and the feeling of time slowing down to a crawl come rushing back. If I close my eyes, I could easily find myself back in that gas station parking lot off Patcher Road in Miami, Mom's body destroyed, her spirit hanging in the air around me without a place to go.

My leg shakes nervously against the wall in front of my stool. I place a hand on my thigh to steady it. A metallic taste fills my mouth and threatens to make its way out. I swallow hard, then reach a hand up to smooth my hair back as if keeping myself presentable will make all of this more normal. It won't, and it's not. Nothing about this is remotely normal. It's surreal. Unspeakable. And it's made worse by the fact that the Callaway family seems to have more than our fair share of tragedies. Asking why seems fruitless, but at this point, it's downright maddening.

Us Callaways don't deserve this. Do we? Have we somehow angered the powers that be? If so, I want to know how to atone. I can't take much more. I want a happy, tranquil existence with a husband and children someday. I want us all to live until old age and die peacefully in our beds, certain we've lived fully and are ready to go. I don't want any part of the accidents and violence my loved ones so far have met at the end of their too-short lives. What terrible ways to go.

The medics knock urgently on the door, and I have a visceral reaction in my body that happens before my mind catches up. I startle, practically leaping off the stool as I scramble to my feet. I stand, then glance down at Grandpa's body. His bald head looks sweet, familiar. From this angle, if I squint my eyes to block out the pool of blood around him, I can imagine that he's laying down for a nap, a newspaper hiked high against his crossed legs. It's the same pose I saw Grandpa strike so often during my childhood. He used to lounge on our sofa, reading the newspaper cover to cover. I remember being a kid and curling up with Grandpa Vern to read the comics. Even as an adult, Grandpa always wrapped presents that he sent me in pages from the comics section. I'm going to miss him so very much.

I should be scared. The men who shot Grandpa Vern could come back to finish the job if they get the idea I was here, too, when it happened. They apparently thought Grandpa was alone. My mind tumbles as I consider the threat to my safety. And to Lottie's. She is such a loose cannon that I'm unsure how to wrangle her into any sort of submission. We'll need to be careful if we're going to make it through this. Hopefully, she's on her way here. But I don't want her walking into a trap.

I hear the sound of heavy footsteps on the stairs outside. As far as I know, the police aren't here yet. I haven't seen any uniformed officers making their way across the lawn with the paramedics. It gives me pause. I wonder if the 9-1-1 operator put a call out for law enforcement. Surely, she did. It seems unwise to send paramedics into a scene like this without armed officers on site to protect them. I'm not sure I should let them in. How do I know these are the good guys?

I'm comforted by a friendly voice on the other side of the door. It's Rags. Thank God.

"Margot, it's me," he says. "It's safe. I'm out here with the paramedics. Can you open the door?"

I don't think I've ever been so glad to hear a particular voice. I'm relieved that Rags is okay. And that he's here to help me get through this. I hate to sound weak, but I need him. I *really* need him. Emotions are high and I realize many people would say it's no time to make any big decisions. I intend to heed that advice. Although I can't help but think Rags and I have an important connection. The way we met by chance and came to Grandpa Vern's just in time to see him together before he was killed has to be more than a coincidence. I'd like to think there's something bigger at work. I cling to that hope, anyway. There has to be more meaning to my life than just getting by long enough to suffer the next catastrophe.

"Rags!" I exclaim as I step over Grandpa's body again

along the path to the front door. I clear my throat, lower my voice, and try to sound strong. "Hold on. I'm on my way."

I take a deep breath as I turn the knob. I hope to God and all that's holy I'm not making a mistake by letting these paramedics in.

When I open the door, Rags is there, his shirt wet with perspiration. He opens his arms and I rush to him, burying my head against his strong chest. The medics move to enter the apartment, but he raises a hand to stop them.

"Give her a minute," he says firmly.

When they stop and stand still, Rags brings his big hand to my head and wraps it around gently as he pulls me to him. Tears fall from my eyes like a Florida summer's rain shower, the source deep and overflowing. I've been alone with my sweet Grandpa's body for at least fifteen minutes, but I haven't shed a single tear until now. I sob and my chest heaves as I let the emotion out. Rags holds me tightly and I can feel the compassion in his touch. He's sad, too. Grandpa Vern was his friend. I'm reminded of the calm, steady presence from earlier this morning when Rags found me near the bench. I'm incredibly thankful that he found me when he did.

The medics are antsy, and I realize that they probably think Grandpa can be saved.

"He's gone," I say with a whimper. "There's no hurry anymore. I'm sure."

They nod, then relax a bit. All three men bow their heads and stand dutifully, giving me the space I need. I appreciate the gesture. It reminds me of how people in the South pull over to allow a funeral procession to pass on the road. The show of respect is gratefully received. Grandpa would want me to be treated nicely. He'd be sick if he knew what I'm going through. Good thing he's not here to witness what's happening. At least, I hope he isn't. I don't know where his spirit is. If Lottie really does have psychic powers, maybe she can communicate with Grandpa somehow. Maybe she can assure him that we'll find a way to be okay. He needs to move on without hanging around here and worrying about us.

When I've cried my eyes out and my breathing has slowed, I lift my head and look into Rags' deep brown eyes.

"Let's go back in," I say. "I'm as ready as I'll ever be."

"Okay," he confirms. "I'm right here, Margot. I'll be with you every step of the way."

I don't ask Rags what happened in his pursuit of the men who shot Grandpa Vern. He doesn't offer an explanation. I feel safer with Rags here. I feel like an explanation can wait. Surely, police officers will arrive any minute. And surely, they'll want to learn what Rags knows. I'll hear the story then.

Rags waves the medics in and they kneel down to tend to Grandpa. They don't look around the condo, which strikes me as a bad move on their part. It seems like they are at risk, and that police officers should really be here with them. The oldest of the medics, who appears to be the leader, takes Grandpa's pulse, then calls the time of death when he doesn't feel one. Hearing the words stings. Rags keeps an arm around me, which I appreciate.

"Shouldn't forensics people be here?" I ask. "To study the crime scene?"

I had pushed it out of my mind, but suddenly

remember the investigators who swarmed the parking lot when Mom was killed. They sectioned the area off with yellow tape as what seemed like dozens of official looking people played their parts. They made notes on clipboards, took photographs, and consulted with each other with ultra serious expressions on their faces. Lottie and I stood nearby, our mother's blood all over us, for what, in hindsight, felt like far too long. Someone should have taken us away from there sooner. Eventually, we ended up with a social worker who put us in a dimly lit, dingy room at the police station where we waited until Grandpa Vern drove up to Miami to get us. The woman was nice. She got us cheeseburgers, which we couldn't stomach, and she tried to distract us with movies and car games. All we could do was sit and stare, at the floor and at each other.

"They should be here soon," Rags says. "It's okay. Every minute feels like a hundred, I know, but we'll get through this. You're doing great."

The oldest medic nods in agreement and gives me a sympathetic look. He feels bad for me. I feel bad for myself. I take another deep breath, I lean into Rags, and I wait.

12

INTERNAL AFFAIRS

Police officers and crime scene investigators do show up, and once they swarm the place, I almost wish I could go back and soak in the peace and quiet a while longer. It's a mad house of activity. The familiar yellow crime tape is draped across the breezeway out front. I'm standing awkwardly with my back pressed against a living room wall when someone officially comes to talk to me. Rags hasn't left my side.

"You in the Navy?" a gruff investigator asks, gesturing to my t-shirt.

He's a crusty looking man who has spent way too much time in the sun. He's almost as tall as Rags, but nowhere near as attractive. His skin is leathery like a crocodile's and his nose is both long and bulbous. At first glance, he seems older. Too old to be working in this field. But upon closer inspection, I don't think he's much beyond forty-five. The years have not been kind.

I nod, although I suspect he already knows the answer to the question. He must have made at least a cursory glance at our records before showing up here. It's what any investigator worth their salt would do.

"Tom Marsh," he says, reaching out to shake my hand. "Hideaway Isle Police Department. I'm the lead investigator on this case. Mind if I ask you a few questions?"

I nod again, my voice failing me when I try to speak. I look up at Rags, who jumps in and introduces himself.

"I'm Rags Bertram," he says, shaking Tom's hand. "I'm a friend of Margot's. And of Vern's."

Rags glances over at Grandpa's body as he says it, a tear forming in his eye. Cameras flash in the background while the team works feverishly to gather evidence. At least they're serious about the job they're here to do. I want them to find Grandpa's killers and bring them to justice. I want to know why they came after an innocent man in the first place. Surely, Grandpa Vern didn't do anything to provoke them.

"Pleased to meet you both," Tom says.

He smells like cigarettes and coffee. I look at him expectantly, without taking the lead. I'm still in a daze. He will have to guide me.

"Is there someplace private we can talk?" Tom asks, glancing around us and into the hallway beyond.

"This is a two bedroom condo," I mutter, gesturing to the bedrooms. "It's not very big, but we can talk there."

"That will be fine," Tom replies, then follows us into the next room.

When I open the door, I'm surprised to see that the room is set up as an office now. I'm drawn to the framed family photos that line the desk and walls, but I hold back. I'll have to look at them another time. Grandpa and

I never made it past the kitchen earlier, which means I haven't been in this room since I left Florida seven years ago. I know from our phone conversations that the space was used as Lottie's. When I look closely, I can see specks of lavender paint at the edges of the pale gray that has been applied recently. The carpet is plush and appears to be new. Grandpa must have remodeled when my sister left last year. Knowing him, he did it to try and move on. It would have broken him every time he glanced in at the lavender walls, knowing that Lottie was out on her own too soon. While he couldn't stop her, he must have known she wasn't ready.

Tom motions for me to sit down first. I place myself in Grandpa's padded leather desk chair. An eggshell cushion sits high on top of the seat, added to help with Grandpa Vern's sciatica, no doubt. Rags pulls up a molded side chair from a corner of the room and offers it to Tom, then sits down in a plush aqua blue armchair nearby, a potted palm close against one side. I don't like how far away Rags is from me. I decide that I'll go over and stand by him if this gets too difficult. We all get as comfortable as possible, then Rags and I look at Tom, eager to get this over with.

"Okay," Tom says. "This is great. Thanks for allowing me to join you here."

"It's my grandpa's condo," I say, nearly tearing up.

I tell myself to hold it together. I don't know how friendly Tom really is. At this point, I think it's wise to be suspicious of everyone until they prove themselves as trustworthy. Who knows what the police around here think of me and my family? They all know about Lottie's company and the boat tour accident, without a doubt.

They're human. I wouldn't blame them if they're already judging me based on my sister's behavior. But it's my duty to remain vigilant.

"Yes, I know," Tom says gently. "Your grandpa is Vernon Callaway, correct?"

"*Was* Vernon Callaway, yes," I say, the corners of my mouth quivering.

"And you're Margot Callaway?"

"That's right."

"Ms. Callaway," Tom says, "Let me begin by saying that I'm very sorry for your loss. This must be excruciating. My heart goes out to you."

My face balls up and I begin to cry. I can't help it. Damn these tears. I nod, covering my face until I can regain my composure. Tom waits respectfully. Maybe he is a good guy. It seems like he genuinely cares, anyway. Rags looks on sympathetically, his face a mask of concern.

"Thank you," I reply. "That's very nice of you."

"It's the truth," Tom says.

I nod again, then pause as I anticipate his next question. For starters, Tom will have to ask us what we were doing here. And whether we saw the men who killed Grandpa Vern. I'm sure he has hundreds of questions in that investigative mind of his. I just hope he will take it slow and easy. I'm already exhausted.

"Listen," Tom says after a moment. "I went to school with your dad. Jon Callaway, right?"

I'm surprised by this revelation. Hideaway Isle is a small place. I guess it makes sense that I'd bump into people who knew Dad. He lived here his entire life, except for the four years spent at college in Gainesville at the University of Florida.

"Yes. You knew him?" I ask.

"We were in school together from Kindergarten all the way through high school graduation," Tom explains. "Jon was a good man. It's a shame what happened to him."

"And to his dad," I add. "And to his wife."

It really is a sad story for us Callaways.

"Of course," Tom replies.

So, he does know our story. Maybe it's better that way. I smile and nod. Rags smiles, too. Maybe Tom Marsh is all right.

"Let's get down to business," Tom says gently. "Do you mind if I record this conversation?"

I shake my head. I knew that was coming. Again, I remember the questions from when Mom died. It's a grueling process, but apparently, a necessary one. Tom pulls a small handheld recorder out of his pants pocket and flicks it on. An indicator light blinks dutifully.

"There," he says. "We're all set."

"What do you need to know?" I ask, speaking louder than usual so my voice can be heard clearly.

"We'll start with the basics," Tom says. "Will you please verify your full name, home address, occupation, and phone number?"

How unusual that Rags and I are going to learn about each other as a result of Grandpa Vern's murder investigation. We'll skip right past the usual first date getting to know each other. Hey, it is what it is.

"Margot Eloise Callaway," I say. "Eloise after my

grandmother, Vern's late wife. She died before I was born."

"I'm sorry," Tom says, taking notes on a lined pad. "I remember hearing about her from your Dad when we were kids. What an honor to be her namesake."

Rags lowers his eyebrows and purses his lips, saddened. "It's a beautiful name," he says.

I smile again, sadly. I'm struck by the way both sadness and beauty exist simultaneously in my life. I guess that's the way it always is, but the juxtaposition is more obvious than ever.

I continue.

"My home address is 4281 Watersound Road, Apartment 8N, Oak Harbor, Washington. My occupation is Naval Flight Officer with the United States Navy."

I rattle off my phone number, eyeing Rags to see if he takes note of the digits. He's smart as a whip. I'm sure he could memorize my complete address and phone number without letting on. And I'll do the same when he mentions his.

"Great," Tom says. "Thank you, Margot. Is it okay if I call you Margot?"

"Yes."

"And, sir," Tom says, turning to Rags. "Will you please provide the same information?"

"Sure thing," Rags replies. "Rags Paul Bertram... and no, Rags isn't a nickname. 21 Coquina Place, Hideaway Isle, Florida. I'm the owner of Nimbus Marina."

Then he lists his phone number. Tom doesn't show any hint of surprise when Rags mentions the marina. Tom must have already known. I'm reminded how Rags said that no one around here knows about his past as a

Navy SEAL. I wonder what lengths he'll go to in order to keep that secret, and why. I certainly won't mention it, but I'm curious. When Rags and I get some downtime together, I intend to ask a few questions.

"Good, thank you," Tom says. "And Margot, please state the name of the gentleman who owns this condo."

I look perplexed, but answer anyway. I guess they need it on the recording.

"Vern… I mean, Vernon Callaway."

"And your relationship with Mr. Callaway, for the record?"

"I'm his granddaughter."

"Thank you."

I wonder if this is the way they usually do things, or if Tom is giving me special treatment since he knew Dad. I suppose answering questions here is better than doing it at the police station. It's more comfortable here. And more private, by a long shot.

"Mr. Bertram," Tom continues, "can I call you Rags?"

"Sure."

"Good. Your relationship to the deceased Mr. Callaway?"

Rags swallows hard. He's a tough guy, but this is getting to him. It only makes me like him more.

"We were friends," Rags explains. "We met last summer when Vern came into the marina to lease a slip for his boat. We got to chatting over the course of a few weeks, then he invited me here to play golf. It's become a weekly occurrence."

"You play golf with Vern every week?"

"Just about. We have a standing date on Friday

mornings. We've only missed a few since last September,"
Rags explains.

"Okay," Tom says, shifting his weight in his chair like
a predator squaring up against its prey.

I don't think Tom means to be aggressive with us. It's
just that he has the ability to show that side when needed.
His body seems to be coiling up instinctively, even though
the tactic isn't needed here.

"Do either of you know why someone would want to
hurt Vern?" he asks pointedly.

Rags and I look at each other. I could share the
information about Lottie. Should I? I'm not sure. Rags
seems like he has something he could share, too. I wonder
if it's about Lottie, or about something different. Probably
something different. But what? I wish I could ask him
without Tom and this recorder listening in.

"My Grandpa is… *was* a good man, if that's what
you're asking," I offer. "He wouldn't have made enemies
of his own."

Tom picks up on the qualifier right away. "How do
you mean, *of his own?* That's an interesting way to say it.
Is there more information you think is relevant?"

I take a deep breath, deciding whether to tell Tom
everything I know. He seems like a genuinely good guy,
even if not the most attractive. His eyes are kind. And I
suppose anyone would look a little haggard if they had to
deal with the kind of stress Tom does on a daily basis. I
imagine it sucks the soul right out of you.

I'll tell him.

"It's… my sister," I say. "Lottie Callaway. She's
nineteen, and she's been in some trouble lately."

"What kind of trouble?" Tom asks, though I assume

he already knows more than I do about my sister's affairs here on the island.

"I actually don't know a lot," I say. "I flew in this morning from Washington State to help Grandpa handle things. He didn't even have a chance to explain what's going on before... well, yeah..."

Rags looks interested. I wonder if Grandpa Vern told him more than he told me. Maybe between the two of us, we can piece things together.

"How about you tell me what you do know?" Tom asks. "Regarding your sister's troubles, that is."

I shrug, my body uncertain.

"I read online about the tour boat accident," I say. "And Grandpa confirmed that Lottie is the real owner of the company. I was shocked. She's just nineteen. A teenager. Practically a child! If you ask me, Lottie doesn't have any business owning that kind of company. She wasn't prepared to handle the responsibility."

Tom makes notes. Rags raises his brows, visibly surprised.

"So, you think people are upset with her?" Tom asks.

I scoff. "Yeah, and that's an understatement," I say, fiddling with the bottom seam of my t-shirt. "If you lost someone in an accident like that, wouldn't you be livid to hear that a teenager owned the company... and was negligent?"

"Was she negligent?"

"I don't know," I say. "I'm just repeating what I read in the news articles. But I'm guessing a lot of people are upset with my sister right now."

Tom keeps a neutral expression. He's clearly been trained not to react unless it serves him in getting a suspect to talk. Again, I don't blame him. It's interesting to observe. I hope I'm not a suspect in his mind. I can't imagine that, but I understand why investigators have to consider all possibilities. If they didn't, they'd miss things and criminals would go free. Besides, there are patterns of human behavior that pan out the majority of the time. Tom has to do his job, even if that means I'm on the receiving end of his inquiry.

"Do you think someone angry with Lottie took their frustrations out on Vernon?" Tom asks, an edge to his tone.

"How should I know?" I ask in reply. "You wanted me to elaborate on what I said, so I did. Lottie's troubles are the only way I could see someone being upset with Grandpa Vern. He's a good man. He simply didn't have enemies."

"I can confirm that, based on the time I've known him," Rags adds.

Tom looks at us both intently, deciding how far to push this right now. He knows there's time to let things unfold. I'm not exactly a flight risk. One call to my commander would have me. Rags isn't either. It isn't like he'd leave his marina. Once ballistics come back, along with the forensics report, Tom will know more. He can question us again then.

"Are we finished here?" I ask. "I don't mean to rush things. I'm happy to come into the station later or another day. But I'm exhausted. I flew in on a red eye last night. It may sound strange under the circumstances, but my body needs some sleep, desperately. Even a short nap would go a long way."

"Understood," Tom says, glancing at his digital wrist

watch. "I have a few more necessary questions, but think we can wrap this up in about ten more minutes. Can you give me that long?"

I agree, then Tom proceeds to run through more of the basics: what we were doing here, what we saw and heard, and whether we might be able to identify the shooters. Rags tells Tom that he left in pursuit, but that all he got was a partial plate number from a large, black SUV with tinted windows.

Tom thanks us for our cooperation and tells us what to expect next as his team processes the condo. He gives me his card, then suggests I find somewhere else to stay, at least for the next couple of nights. I hate to go because this is where Lottie knows to find me, but I realize I must. I take note of my sister's phone number from Grandpa's list on the wall, then I make my way through the forensics people, bend down over Grandpa Vern's lifeless body, and gently kiss him goodbye.

13

STAND BY ME

Rags offers to let me crash at his place for as long as I like. He tells me he has a cottage on Coquina Place with a spare bedroom. I remember the address. I might still check into a hotel later, but first, I need that nap. I'm bone tired, as if Grandpa's death has depleted every last drop of my energy reserves. A person can only take so much. I agree to take Rags up on his offer, and I ride along wearily as he drives me to his island home.

My suitcase is still in Chevelle's car. I'll have to retrieve it from her soon. I also need to call my commander and, as a courtesy, let him know I've been questioned by local police. I don't much care about either task at this moment though. I am so very tired. I decide to let everything slide for at least a few hours. It's afternoon here in Florida, but still morning on Whidbey Island. One step at a time. Sleep first.

"Are you hungry?" Rags asks as we pull into his short driveway.

His house is adorable. It's the picture perfect island

cottage with a wide porch that covers the entire front of the house and sky blue shutters that flank stately windows. A wooden front door looks handcrafted, while a black metal pendant light hangs from the porch ceiling just above the entrance. Out of nowhere, a rush of emotion hits me. I can't immediately identify the feelings, but seeing this quaint little home stirs something deep within me. It's the kind of home I could see myself living in. Like Goldilocks, this one seems like it would fit me just right. I don't need a sprawling mansion. Give me a nice porch, some flowers out front, and a space to plant my own garden, and I'm golden. For me, it's about quality rather than quantity. I'm beginning to see that Rags shares my sensibilities. I'm beginning to imagine what the two of us might be like together.

"I don't know about you, but my stomach is growling something fierce," Rags says. "That breakfast burrito isn't holding me anymore."

"Yeah," I say, snapping out of my daydream. "Sorry, I'm a little out of it. I don't feel hungry, but I guess I should eat."

Rags gets out and shuts the driver door of the Jeep behind him. The officer assigned to monitor me hasn't arrived yet. I wonder if I should worry, but I don't. Not really. I feel safe with Rags. Even though I've only known him for a matter of hours, I trust that he won't let anything happen to me.

"I can make us something," he says as he opens my door and extends his hand to help me out of the vehicle.

Normally, I'd give a man hell for opening doors for me and treating me like some hapless little girl. With Rags, today, I don't feel that way about it. I warm under the glow of his attention, and not just because we're in the South Florida heat. Maybe it's because of what just happened with Grandpa. That situation is a lot to take in. But I think Rags would have the same effect on me under any circumstance. There's something different about this man. His mouth. His strong shoulders. The way he glides through the air when he walks. He's getting to me.

"You cook?" I ask.

"I try," he says with a smile. "I'll let you be the judge as to whether I'm any good at it."

I smile back, although I feel a little guilty doing so. Grandpa Vern has just been killed. It doesn't seem right to feel anything but sadness and grief, and fear for our safety. I don't know what the shooters want or why they came after Grandpa. And I don't know how Lottie figures in. There's much to be concerned about until we get to the bottom of this mess. I believe Rags will look after me, but it's just so much.

Rags notices the happiness fall away from my face and seems to share my sentiment. He relaxes his expression, a more serious air between us.

"I don't know how to act," I say as I take his hand and step out of the Jeep onto the concrete driveway, suddenly conscious of the blood on my Navy t-shirt. I'll need to change into something clean. "It feels wrong to be happy right now. I hope you won't take that personally because I'm enjoying your company."

Rags smiles again, unable to keep his mouth fixed in a completely serious way. He leads me towards the front porch, letting the vehicle door close behind us. The sidewalk is lined with meticulously maintained tropical plants, and I wonder if Rags takes care of the lush

landscaping himself. The thought gives me hope that
maybe there is a garden out back. Maybe gardening is
something we could do together... someday.

"I get it," he replies. "You don't have to explain to me.
I want to do right by Vern. I guess I'm torn between
knowing he'd want you-- *us*-- to be happy and
maintaining the right level of thoughtfulness to show him
respect."

"Exactly," I agree.

"I'll follow your lead," Rags says. "You do what feels
right to honor your Grandpa. If that means we stay
serious for a while, we'll do it. If you want to loosen up
and let things happen... like he suggested... then we'll do
that, too."

I smile big now, as I step onto the porch and admire
the detailing on the front of the house. There's a pale
pink ceramic plaque in the shape of a starfish from the
Historic Florida Keys Foundation that designates the
house as a historic property, and a brass door knocker in
the shape of a dolphin decorates the entryway in classic
Florida island style. This cottage is cute as a button. It
could easily make the cut to be featured in a glossy home
and garden magazine. I can hardly wait to see the
inside.

I'm a sucker for historic homes, ever since my happy
childhood days of living in the two story beauty my
parents owned on Kestrel Cay. I've always sort of thought
I'd buy an old house and fix it up one day. I'm not sure
when that could actually happen given my choice to
pursue a career in the military. Maybe when I retire from
the Navy. If I stay in long enough to retire. I could
separate from active duty service sooner if I wanted to. I

wonder if Rags did the remodeling work on this place himself. It appears the updates are recent.

I haven't forgotten what Grandpa said about letting things happen with Rags. In fact, those were practically his last words. I wonder if fate brought Rags and me together, just in time for Grandpa Vern to give his blessing. If so, who am I to push that good fortune away?

"You're sweet," I say bashfully, appreciative of him letting me take the lead.

I've been on my share of dates. I've hooked up with guys, and I've had long term boyfriends. In fact, my last boyfriend, Jordan Delaney, was another NFO in training with me at Naval Air Station Pensacola. We might still be together if we hadn't been assigned to squadrons on opposite sides of the United States. I'm sexually experienced enough to know what I like. I *think* I'm decent in bed based on the feedback I've received. But my love life is not an area that I feel particularly competent in. I'm like a metaphorical baby deer, all frozen in the headlights and stumbling on wobbly legs. I've learned that it's best if I don't try too hard, or else it gets even worse. I choke on my words, spill things on my clothes, and steer towards dreadfully boring topics of conversation. It's embarrassing.

I'd like to meet the man of my dreams and get married someday. I'd even like to become a mom with children of my own, although I admit I've been fearful about the prospect of dying and leaving them alone like my parents left me. That trauma is hard to shake. Still, I've allowed myself to remain hopeful that a fulfilling family life could happen for me. I always figured the details would work themselves out when it was time, so I focused on my career in the Navy. *That* is more predictable. Orderly. Even though much of what takes place in the Navy is beyond my control-- base assignments, to name a big one-- there are established parameters that allow me to predict with a reasonable level of certainty what is in store for me. At a minimum, those parameters let me narrow the possibilities down to a few solid bets. Love, by comparison, is an entirely different animal. It's a wild and unruly thing, prone to sweep one up and away against their will then leave them battered and bruised, worse for the wear. I hope to have the courage to one day throw caution to the wind and step into that unpredictable whirlwind. I'm just not sure I'm there yet. I wasn't expecting to even have to consider it.

As Rags turns his key in the door, a deep bark booms from inside the house.

"You have a dog?" I ask, though I instantly find myself thinking that Rags is definitely the dog type.

"Yeah, that's Captain," he says. "Don't laugh, but his full name is Captain America. I call him Cap for short. He's a good big boy."

So, Rags is a superhero fan. Noted.

"Is Cap friendly?" I ask, laughing.

I like dogs, but after the few days I've had, I feel the need to ask.

"Very," Rags says. "He's a black lab. A big ol' baby. His bark sounds menacing, but you're good with him once he knows you're with me."

"I'm sure there's a joke about America's Ass here somewhere," I offer, demonstrating my knowledge of the Marvel Universe and specifically, the Avengers movies.

Something else we have in common. I love those movies.

"Right?" Rags says. "I've been telling Cap I could dress him up for Halloween and let the ladies get a squeeze."

We laugh together. It feels good.

As I follow Rags inside his house, I'm overwhelmed by how cozy and comforting the place is. Hardwood floors gleam against colorful paint on the walls, while wooden shutters and shiplap accents provide finishing touches. The furnishings are colorful, too, and they're island themed. Solid wood mixes expertly with wicker, rattan, and leather. The vibe in the house is decidedly masculine, but the decor is so nice it almost seems like a professional interior designer made the selections. It's beautiful. So beautiful, it chokes me up. It feels like... home. More so than any other place I've been. It's the perfect blend of my island heritage and my modern adult sensibilities.

"Rags, this place is gorgeous," I mutter. "I'm impressed."

He smiles in return. "Good. I'm glad you think so. I've put a lot of blood, sweat, and tears into fixing it up. I like to stay busy. You know, do something productive."

"You've done an incredible job."

"It was easy, given what I had to work with. This place is a gem."

I nod, then squat down to greet Cap, who is a bundle of energy. He's a young dog. Probably little more than a year old. He still looks like an adolescent, all gangly and eager. He's a good looking boy with a shiny coat and sparkly white teeth. I pat him on the head playfully. He reminds me of the lab we had when I was a kid. Marina was a deep black, just like Cap. She was a true friend. One of the best parts of my childhood. She died of old age not long after we lost Dad, which hit us hard. Come to think of it, there's a strange synchronicity in the fact that my dog was named Marina, since Rags owns a marina. And I swear, the two pups could be siblings, they look so similar.

"Hey, there, handsome boy," I coo. "Pleased to meet you, Cap."

Cap practically smiles up at me. Rags seems pleased. He runs a strong hand down Cap's back as the dog wriggles with delight.

"He likes you," Rags says.

"I like him, too," I reply. "When I was a kid, we had a dog that looked so much like Cap, she could have been his sister."

"Whoa," Rags says. "How cool. What was her name?"

"Marina," I say, opening my eyes wide. "How crazy is that? We called her Mari for short."

Rags squats next to me, then reaches over and smooths my hair back. It's the same motion I use to tend to errant strands, which makes the gesture all the more intimate. He's seen me do it that way. He's paying attention.

My cheeks flush as a wave of heat moves through me. Not sure how to handle it, I stand and focus on the nap I desperately need.

"You said I could crash for a while?" I ask. "I really want to get some sleep."

"Absolutely," Rags says. "Can I make you something to eat first?"

"How about the nap first, then dinner would be great."

"You've got it," he confirms. "Want to get cleaned up?"

He points to the blood on my shirt.

"You know, I do, but I don't think I have the energy to shower. The blood is all dried at this point, anyway. And besides, my suitcase is in my friend's car."

"No worries. I'll take care of it while you nap," Rags says. "Toss your clothes outside the bedroom door and I'll wash and dry them."

That sounds fantastic right now. I want to be cared for. Doted on.

"You'd do that?" I ask.

"It would be my pleasure," he says, and I believe him.

Rags shows me to the guest bedroom where I slide out of my bloody clothes and into the plush bed. A ceiling fan with wide blades circles slowly overhead and it reminds me of a Navy aircraft. The motion is comforting. My body responds by falling into a deep and peaceful sleep.

14

RETRIEVERS

For the first time in a long while, I dream of my mother. We're on the sandy beach near our Kestrel Cay house. The one from my happy childhood memories. She's in front of me, wearing a wide brimmed straw hat and a flowing white dress over a red bikini, her long chestnut hair dancing in the breeze as she smiles and twirls like a ballerina on one foot. There's magic in the air. For a moment, I feel like I'm a kid again. And she has come back for me. My wonderful, loving mother. I've missed her so very much.

Mom always did have a physicality about her that made people take notice. Both men and women seemed to perk up when she was nearby. She knew how to flirt to get what she wanted, but it wasn't just that. She projected confidence, even when she didn't actually feel sure of herself inside. I think being able to turn on that charisma drew people to her. It made them want to be seen by her. To be recognized.

I sometimes wish I'd inherited Mom's magnetism. She had it in spades.

Her body was attractive in a full on supermodel kind of way. I knew it from the time I was very young. Mom had long, slim yet muscular legs, a shapely waist leading to an ample bust, and an elegant neck that made her mane of wavy hair that much more pleasing to the eye. She stayed tanned at just the right level without becoming leathery. Maybe that deterioration due to sun damage would have happened when she was older, but as it was, Mom left this Earth with her youthful beauty intact. Her rich brown hair never turned white. Her skin never wrinkled beyond the subtle laugh lines around her mouth, and those were hard earned from years of smiling broadly. I don't think she saw them as a flaw.

I blink my eyes as I stare at her now, the image so vivid that it almost seems too realistic to be a dream. Gulls squawk overhead as the water's edge rhythmically recedes then returns, gradually pulling towards low tide. I can practically smell the salt from the sea, the sunscreen on my own tan shoulders. In my memories of being at the beach with Mom, I'm a child. In this dream, I'm my present-day self, all grown up, though still wounded from the pain and suffering I've experienced. I wonder if I'll ever truly heal, if my emotional skin will ever be restored to its previous durability, functional by means other than me running away from everything I love.

"Mom?" I ask quizzically. "Is it really you?"

For some strange reason, I feel like this is more than a dream. Like Mom is really here, and that we're connecting somehow through time and space.

"Margot," she says, reaching her delicate hand my way. "Come. Dance with me."

I'm hesitant, but I consider it. Her voice is the same. It's rich and lovely, a powerful mezzo soprano. I had forgotten the fine details of her face, of the way she moved, of the feel of her skin against mine. A stab of longing hits me and it hurts to have forgotten. I feel like a bad daughter. I wonder if Lottie remembers Mom any better. Probably not. Since she was younger, if anything, she probably remembers even less. I'm struck by what a shame that is. Mom grew two human beings in her body, raised them to ages nineteen and twelve before she had to go, and those daughters don't even fully remember her. I'm saddened by this realization, but I also feel like Mom doesn't want me to be.

"Don't be sad," she implores. "Dance with me."

My resistance beginning to wane, I look down and see that Marina, the old black lab I was just telling Rags about, is here with us. Mari looks vivacious as ever, her black fur shiny and thick. She joins Mom at the edge of the surf and barks gleefully, standing on her hind legs and practically bouncing as Mom moves to her imaginary beat. I'm so glad to see them both. Their company is too enticing, too pleasurable to ignore.

I let my guard down and give in. I walk towards Mom and Mari, twirling around and around, bouncing, leaping, and letting my body move more freely than I have since I was a kid. I find that I don't need to hear what Mom does. We're synchronized by default. Maybe we always were. The joy is all encompassing. In this simple dream, it feels like something deep inside of me is made whole. Like maybe I can go on to face the troubles with Lottie.

Maybe I can grieve Grandpa Vern and get through it. Maybe I can remain open to what Puck has to say. And maybe I can forgive. Heal. Move forward with an open heart. Move forward with Rags, if fate should deem it the proper course.

"Mom, I'm so happy to see you," I say, tears in my eyes. "I can't believe it."

I swear, it feels like the tears are streaming down my face and onto Rags' guest bedroom pillow as they fall in my dream. Mom stops dancing long enough to embrace me. She scoops me into her, wrapping her arms around me so tightly I think I might break. But it feels superb. It feels like it used to. We're together again, just like we used to be. Having Dad and Lottie with us would be even better, but I won't complain. I'll take what I can get and will enjoy every second of this private time with Mom. Mari slows down to lean hard against my leg, her version of an embrace. I pat the top of her silky head, then close my eyes and soak it all in. I have questions-- so many questions-- for Mom, but I don't want to spoil this reunion. I've never felt like this before... like I'm actually with Mom. Not just dreaming about Mom, but like I'm *with* her. We're together somehow. We're communicating.

Suddenly, I hear panting and scratching. The sound interrupts the dream experience, which makes me angry. I don't want to leave Mom. Not now. Not ever. I look at Mari, but the scratching isn't coming from her. She's standing by Mom and me, wagging her tail and looking up at us with her wise eyes.

"What's that sound?" I ask, searching Mom's face for an answer.

She turns her head towards the sea, and I can feel her

slipping away.

"No!" I shout. "Don't go. Forget it. I don't need to know about the sound. Mom, come back!"

It's no use. The scratching is now accompanied by whining. It's definitely a dog, and if it's not Mari, it must be Cap. It sounds like he's scratching on the bedroom door. He wants to get in. He wants to wake me up. And it's working.

I cry out for Mom again. "Please," I beg. "Do you have a message for me? Or Lottie? What did you come to tell me?"

In a flash, Mom's face is right in front of mine. Her button eyes swimming with emotion.

"I'm so sorry," she says. "That's it. I'm sorry."

"Sorry for what?" I ask. "The dream coming to an end? Dying when we still needed you? Leaving me and Lottie alone in the world, both of us thrown into the deep end, unable to swim?"

She's fading away, as is Mari. The scratching and whining at the door intensifies, Cap frantic now. His anxiety feeds mine. I want to run to somehow capture her, even though doing so would be like trying to capture fog. Or the golden light from the morning sunrise. Like many of the other amazing things in the world, Mom's presence is elusive, fleeting. She can't be captured.

Mom looks at me wistfully and makes one last statement.

"For the things you'll find out, Margot. I'm truly sorry."

And then she's gone.

I jerk awake, feeling the jolt of the unfamiliar room and the distraught dog at the door. My face is wet with tears. Soaking wet. I sit up in bed, then look down and remember that I'm wearing nothing but my bra and panties. *Right.* Rags put my clothes in the wash. I have no idea how long I've been asleep, or whether the clothes are done. I pick up my phone from the nightstand and look at the time. It reads six thirty-three, but that doesn't help much. I'm so exhausted and disoriented after the dream that I have trouble calculating the difference in time zones. I don't remember what time it was when I got into this bed.

Cap continues to paw at the door, fuming.

"Cap?" I call. "What is it, boy?"

He yowls, apparently determined to get my attention. Groaning, I stand and open the door, using the quilt from the bed to cover myself. Cap bounds into the bedroom, licking my hand and wiggling all over the place. It's remarkable how much he looks like my Mari. I bend down, smoothing the hair on the top of his head.

"It's okay, boy," I say. "You're a good boy, aren't you?"

He smiles up at me, his wide mouth giving him human qualities. Maybe the smile is my imagination. Whatever the case, Cap seems calm now that he's roused me.

"Where's your dad?" I ask, ducking my head out into the hallway to look for Rags.

The light in the cottage is dim. It seems later than six thirty. Maybe my phone didn't sync up properly with the local cell site and is still displaying Whidbey Island time. I scoot into the living room, holding the quilt around my body with one hand and smoothing my hair back with the other. One feel of my unruly head tells me that smoothing my hair isn't going to help much. I sigh and pull the band free from the back, letting my curly locks fall freely. I suppose Rags has already seen me at my worst. What will a little unruly hair matter? Maybe he'll even like it this way.

A quick glance around the room tells me that Rags isn't here. Strange. I wonder where he went. On the counter in the kitchen are my clothes, freshly laundered and folded. I grab them up, holding them with the same hand that's keeping the quilt around me.

"Where did your dad go?" I ask Cap.

Before Cap can respond, a white piece of paper falls from the counter onto the floor. It has something scribbled on the front. A note.

MARGOT,

I had to go out for a little while. Be back soon. Dinner is in the oven. An officer is stationed outside to keep watch. Make yourself at home.

XO,

R.

I SMILE AS I READ. HE'S A SWEETIE. NOT OVER THE TOP, but enough to intrigue me. I suspect that Rags Bertram is a man who would take excellent care of me. Not because he had to in some old-fashioned way that would render me a damsel in distress, but because he'd want to. I feel my cheeks pink as I think about it. I blush, considering what it would be like if Rags was my own.

Cap whimpers again, directing my attention to the oven. That stinker. Did he wake me up so I'd give him table scraps? I glance down and ask him as much. He practically nods. I chuckle as I open the oven and pull out a warming tray that looks like something they'd serve on a fancy dinner cruise. The aroma fills me top to bottom as I take it in, lifting the lid to find roast chicken, mashed potatoes, asparagus, and macaroni and cheese. It all appears to be made from scratch. A loaf of bread sits at the back of the tray, boasting pretty x-shaped indentations from the pan it was baked in. I'm ravenously hungry. A glass filled with ice cubes sits on the counter nearby, strategically placed next to a pitcher of tea. I pour some for myself and take a big sip. It's lightly sweetened and delicious.

Still wearing the quilt, I plop myself down on a dining room chair and dig into the feast Rags has prepared for me. The food feels like love going in, washed down with the best tea I've ever tasted. It's all so decadent and I'm so hungry, I almost forget the dream and whatever Mom is sorry for. I give Cap a few scraps because I'd be a monster not to. He licks his lips, satisfied, and I copy the motion.

When I'm done, I clean my dishes and get dressed. I'd love a shower, but that seems too presumptuous, so I decide to wait. I use a hand towel in the guest bathroom to clean myself up as well as I can. I'm blotting my freshly washed face and running a hand through my hair when my phone rings.

It's Chevelle. I've put her off long enough. We need to talk about Puck. I need my suitcase. I also need to tell her about Rags and Grandpa Vern, and have her help me figure out what to do with Lottie. Most of all, I need my friend if I'm going to get through this.

I pick up the phone, then invite her over.

15

PEACEKEEPING

I t takes Chevelle less than twenty minutes to find Rags' house and park Knick Knack out front. I consider texting Rags to let him know I have company, but something tells me it isn't necessary. I'm standing in the open front door, Cap stationed dutifully at my side, when Chevelle approaches the front of the house. She has the handle of my suitcase in one hand and she's rolling it up the driveway, suspiciously eyeing the police car parked against the curb. I wave her in and give her a look that says I'll explain everything soon enough. She seems curious, but satisfied.

"Ooh-*wee*," Chevelle says as she steps inside Rags' cottage and glances around, her wide eyes surveying the property.

"Yeah, it's a charmer," I reply. "Make yourself comfortable. I swear, I've totally lost track of time today. It's nearly dark, and I thought it was six something."

"Yeah," she says simply.

It's unusual for her to be so brief. Chevelle usually has

plenty to say. As I go to shut the door, I notice that she left her car running.

"Hey," I say. "Are you feeling okay? You left Knick Knack running out there. That isn't like you, Chev…"

Her face drops and I instantly know what she's up to.

"Dammit, Chevelle. He's in the car, isn't he?"

She nods, only a little ashamed of herself. I've never seen my friend so willing to interfere in my life. It's frustrating. She has no idea what I've been through today or what I'm dealing with, yet she wants to force a damn family reunion on me. We don't even know if Puck's claims are legitimate. He and I might not be family at all.

"He wanted to come," she offers, as if that makes it okay. "He's been waiting all day for another chance to talk to you. He took the evening off work and everything."

I step out front again, ducking down to see Puck below the roofline of Chevelle's little red car. His eyes meet mine, a mix of excitement and reluctance. I wave him in with a sweeping motion.

"Come on, Puck," I mouth. "Get your ass in here."

It's strange. He may turn out to be my older brother, but I still feel like the oldest sibling, ready to take the lead and boss him around. Maybe I'm just used to the role. I should probably be careful not to overpower him. I tell myself to give the man a chance. At least, his claims of being my biological brother can be settled relatively quickly with a DNA test. Of all the dilemmas in my life at present, that one will have a certain answer. In fact, I ought to just do a test and get it over with. One thing to cross off the list.

Puck turns off the ignition and climbs out of the little car.

"I don't want to intrude," he says, glancing at the front of the cottage, then at the police cruiser. "I'm happy to wait for Chevelle in the car."

"Is that what you really want?" I ask. "Because if it's not, you have to speak up."

Cap has returned to my side. It's as if he's decided to adopt me. I wasn't expecting him to take to me like this. Granted, I wasn't expecting to meet Rags or Cap at all. But I appreciate their kindness. They make me feel special. And like everything else about Rags and his cottage, Cap makes me feel at home.

"No," Puck says reluctantly. "I'd like to talk to you some more. If you have the time and energy. I know you're tired from your trip, and this is… well, it's a lot."

He doesn't even know about Grandpa Vern.

Puck puts both hands in his pockets and sort of rocks on his heels as he talks. His awkwardness makes me feel bad for him. Puck is not smooth and self-assured like Rags. I suppose Puck does seem somehow like a brother. He gives me brother vibes. Huh. Interesting.

I nod.

"Hey," I say. "I took a nap a little while ago and had a dream about my mom… my Annie."

"Oh, yeah?" Puck asks, his face lighting up.

He really believes that my Annie and his are one and the same. It's evident by the sincerity of his response. I can't help but like the guy, despite my inclination not to. I realize it isn't Puck I'm mad at. It's the situation. I wish I wasn't having to deal with some brother I didn't know I had. What should I call him? Estranged? Abandoned?

Mom's love child? I don't know the details yet. I should reserve judgment. It's just that Puck's very existence, if he's a blood relative, will make me see Mom in an entirely different light. It will mean that the Mom I thought I knew was a lie. A fake. How am I supposed to come to terms with that?

"Yeah," I say. "And it seemed real. Strangely so."

He practically beams.

"That's how it is when I dream of her," he explains. "And sometimes, I think I hear her voice in my head, even while I'm awake."

I nod.

"Lottie apparently dreams about her, too, although she and I haven't talked about it. Our Grandpa Vern told me."

"Say," Puck suggests, "do you happen to have a picture of her? Of... Annie?"

I do, on my phone, and in one of my photo albums on Facebook, although those are set to private so only my Facebook friends can view them.

"Do you have a picture of your Annie?" I ask Puck, avoiding his question.

"Yes. I mean, I do now," he says. "I didn't. Until recently, when my dad-- I mean my grandfather, Herbert-- gave me a few old photos."

"So, I suppose we could compare them. If I had a picture," I muse. "Are you ready for that?"

"Hell, yeah, I'm ready," he says, showing more of his true personality than I've seen thus far. "Are you?"

His enthusiasm is infectious.

"I don't know," I say hesitantly. "I do have some photos of her on my phone and on Facebook. It feels scary, but hey, it's just looking at a few snapshots, right? Ignoring this won't make it go away."

Puck smiles broadly, taking his hands out of his pockets.

"I've always wanted a sibling," he proclaims, his white teeth gleaming as they peek through his lips.

"Or two?" I ask. "If you turn out to be my big brother, that means you'll have to help me with Lottie. You do realize that, right? And dealing with her isn't going to be easy. She's a wild child."

A somber expression spreads over his face, like he thinks I expect him to be ultra-serious. I don't. Although, I guess Lottie's situation is pretty serious.

"I'll be there for you in any way I can," he replies. "I have Chely, my girlfriend, and our baby who is due soon. Oh, and my grandfather. But there's room for more family in my life. You have my word, Margot. If I'm your brother, you can count on me."

I kind of like that idea. I smile, then Puck allows his face to lighten, too.

"Okay, then," I say. "Come inside and we'll do this. Chevelle is apparently determined to make it happen. Let's not keep her waiting any longer."

"Okay!" he exclaims.

We go inside, followed closely by Cap, who wags his tail happily. I introduce the dog to Puck and Chevelle, who each stroke his head and talk to him cheerfully. Cap seems proud to have visitors. He moves between us like a good host, tending to his guests.

Puck trails behind me as I go to the kitchen table. We each take a seat and place our phones on the table in front of us.

"Oh, we're doing this?" Chevelle asks, snapping her fingers in the air for dramatic effect. "Just like that?"

"It's what you want, isn't it?" I ask. "You want it so much that you'd spring this man on me the minute I stepped off the plane."

"Margot, don't be mad," Chevelle says. "I want what's best for you."

"Yeah, Margot, please don't be mad," Puck adds.

"What was I supposed to say when he called me and told me his story?" Chevelle asks. "If the tables were turned, you would have done the same thing."

"Would I?" I ask.

Chevelle sticks her lower lip out, pretending to pout. Using her index fingers, she pulls her lower eyelids down so that the combination makes her look like a sad puppy dog. I try to keep a straight face, but I can't help but laugh. I shake my head, then pull my friend into the chair beside me, forcing her to move her hands away from her face.

"Stop it," I say, laughing out loud.

She sits, then claps her hands gleefully. Cap lets out a happy whimper in response. Maybe this isn't so bad. Maybe it's what's supposed to happen. I take a deep breath and steel myself. If my Annie is Puck's Annie, we'll know it the minute we compare pictures. Even given the time and age difference, a person doesn't change much. Not in the face. The eyes. The smile. I'll know Mom if Puck shows me a picture of her.

"How do we want to proceed?" Puck asks.

He's eager. He has nothing to lose and everything to gain. Puck knew his parents abandoned him, and he's spent most of his life wishing to learn about them and solve the mystery of who they were and why they left. Finding out more about who his mother was would be a huge break for him. A gift. For me, on the other hand, not so much.

I take another deep breath.

"You look first," I suggest. "I'll pull up a picture. You look, and let me know if she resembles your Annie. Annie Reed, you say?"

"That's right. Go ahead."

I open the Facebook app on my phone and navigate to the album that I've titled Old Pictures of Friends and Family. I open it, selecting a picture of Mom, Lottie, and me that was taken in Miami Beach not long before she died. I'm holding up the peace sign, pushing my lips out to try and look cool. Lottie is grinning like the innocent little girl she was back then, her face relaxed and fresh. Mom stands at the back with her arms around us, clearly proud of her girls. A pang of guilt hits me and I wonder if I should show Puck this picture. If Mom is his mom, too, and she really did abandon him, it will surely hurt for him to see how connected we were. I close the photo and look for another one, but they're all essentially the same. Mom was very connected to Lottie and me. I won't be able to hide that fact.

"Any one will do," Puck says, unable to hide his anticipation.

I nod, then close my eyes for a few seconds. *Here goes nothing*, I think to myself, then I enlarge the Miami Beach photo and thrust my phone towards Puck. Chevelle looks on curiously, her eyes nearly as wide as my own.

"Well?" I ask when Puck doesn't speak right away.

"Don't leave me hanging. Does it look like the same Annie?"

His lip quivers ever so slightly at one corner, and his face begins to ball up. He opens his mouth, but no words come out. He's speechless. Literally, speechless.

"It's her, isn't it?" I ask.

"Mm hmm," Chevelle mutters, unable to remain quiet.

"Show me one of your pictures," I command, slapping Puck on the wrist.

He shakes his head, suddenly talking too much.

"Maybe this was a bad idea," Puck blurts, rising from the table and fidgeting nervously. "I think I should leave. I'll... I'll call a rideshare... Or I'll walk. That's it. Nothing is far on this island. Or... I'll call Chely to come pick me up."

Chevelle moves to steady him.

"Puck Reed," she says firmly, "this is what you've been waiting for. You aren't going anywhere. Not yet."

I nod my agreement.

"Just do it," I instruct. "Like ripping off a band-aid. Show me one of your pictures."

Puck looks to one side, then quickly to the other as if he's searching for an escape. He chokes up, the anxiety spilling out of him, until finally, he flips through his own phone and shows us a picture.

My heart beats like a marching band in my chest when I see it. It's Mom. *My Annie.* Puck's Annie is my Annie. I don't know how it can be, but it's her. She's younger in his photo, her face thinner, her features softer and less angular. She's wearing high-waisted jeans and a yellow crop top, leaning back against a brick wall. It's definitely her.

"Where did you get that?" I ask, somewhat surprised that my voice works.

Puck swallows hard.

"I…"

"Enough with the theatrics," I say, meaner than I should. "Who gave you that picture?"

Puck complies, almost like he wants a sister who will boss him around. Maybe he's been lacking such a personality to whip him into shape.

"My… my father… I mean, grandfather. Herbert Finley."

"And how did he know Annie Callaway?" I ask.

Puck shoves a hand through his hair and taps his foot against the wood floor as he musters the needed courage. His words hit me like daggers as he speaks, a jolt to the system.

"She's his daughter. Born Annie Finley, she became Annie Reed while married to my dad…"

I finish Puck's sentence, my mind catching up to what my heart knew to be true the moment he made the connection at breakfast this morning.

"And then she became Annie Callaway while married to mine."

I have a brother. Wow. A brother that my mom apparently abandoned when he was a young child. Not to mention, she must have also cut ties with her parents. I'm not sure how to make sense out of this, but I suppose I'll find a way.

I reach out and take Puck's hand.

"You're… my little sister," he says. "The little sister

I've always wanted. This is one of the best days of my entire life. You have no idea how happy this makes me."

Chevelle and Cap smile in response. I grab Chevelle's hand, too, and I'll admit, this feels like a positive beginning. We're holding hands, tears in our eyes and happy expressions on our faces when we hear a commotion outdoors.

16

OPEN THE DOOR

I listen closely to rustling and stomping, a car door slamming, and then another. It sounds like a fight is about to break out in the front yard. A man's voice booms, his emotions running high. It takes me a minute, but I recognize Rags' voice. I stand and move to the paned glass window closest to the front door to get a view. Rags is yelling at the police officer assigned to me as he rushes towards the front door. He must be worried about the strange car in the driveway. Apparently, he thinks the cop is falling down on the job. I open the door to greet Rags just as he pulls on the handle, ready to burst in. When he sees me, his gnarled up face relaxes with relief.

"Margot!" Rags exclaims, taking me into his arms. He doesn't hesitate or try to hide his affection for me. "You're ok?"

I hear Chevelle let out another *ooh-wee* in the background.

"Yeah, I'm fine," I say, squeezing him back. "No need to worry. I invited a friend over, and she brought, well…

it's a long story. Come on in and I'll tell you all about it. I hope you don't mind."

Rags let out a big sigh.

"Of course, I don't mind. It just scared me for a minute when I saw the strange car in the driveway."

He steps back out the door and waves apologetically to the officer at the curb.

"I should have called or texted to let you know," I say. "I didn't even consider that you'd be worried about me like this."

He pulls me to him again, wrapping an arm around my waist.

"I'm not usually so jumpy," Rags says. "After this morning, I'm… rattled…"

"What happened this morning?" Chevelle asks, prompting me to turn my attention back to her.

I take Rags by the hand and lead him to the dining table where Chevelle and Puck are seated. He pulls the door all the way closed, then gives Cap a quick scratch behind the ears before following me. It feels as natural as anything to hold his hand. To lead him around the cottage. To be enveloped in his embrace.

"Rags, meet my long time best friend, Chevelle Mooney, and my… I guess I'll call him my new brother, Puck Reed," I say.

"*New* brother?" Rags asks.

"Yeah, I just found out today," I say. "Nothing official yet, but we compared photos. We have the same mother."

"Wow," Rags replies, sitting down in the chair beside me as Cap leans on his leg.

Those two are clearly buddies. Man's best friend, for sure.

Puck reaches a hand out to greet Rags.

"Pleased to meet you, sir."

It's funny to hear Puck address Rags that way. Puck is older. But Rags has a far more commanding presence.

"The pleasure is mine," Rags says, his eyes bright.

He turns to Chevelle.

"Good to meet you, too," Rags says as he takes Chevelle's hand and shakes it lightly. "Any friend of Margot's is a friend of mine."

Chevelle smiles and then pretends to fan her face.

"Indeed," she says. "Um, um, um."

I laugh.

"You'll have to excuse my friend," I say to Rags, while winking at Chevelle. "She can't seem to keep herself together when in the presence of a good-looking man."

Rags blushes. It's hard for me to believe that a man like him gets embarrassed, but apparently, he does.

"You think I'm good-looking?" he asks me, placing his hand on top of mine on the table.

Now I blush.

"Wasn't that obvious?" I ask, lowering my gaze.

Puck coughs, uncomfortable with our flirting. Chevelle takes it in stride. In fact, she seems to be enjoying it.

"Okay, Margot," she says. "Sounds like you have explaining to do in both directions. How about you get to it?"

I chuckle, then nod my agreement. This conversation is insane. Just twenty-four hours ago-- hell, even twelve hours ago-- I couldn't have imagined it. It's amazing how life can truly turn on a dime.

"Things are happening so fast that I can hardly keep up," I say. "It's been quite a day."

"Try," she implores.

"Fine," I say. "I'll start with what's easiest."

"Wise choice," Rags says.

He's enjoying this. I get the idea he's proud to meet more of my people. I shift my weight in the chair, turning towards Rags. He leaves his hand on mine, weaving his fingers through. The sensation sends tingles up and down my spine. I narrow my eyes as the warm, delicious feeling washes over me.

"You alright over there?" he says, smiling.

I sit up straight and force myself to focus. I tell myself to talk now and savor the feeling of Rags' skin on mine later.

"I'm good," I say. "I'll catch you up first."

"You're saying I'm easy?" Rags asks jovially.

He leans towards me and I imagine myself meeting his lips with my own. Damn, this man is alluring.

"Are you?" I ask.

Chevelle pretends to fan herself again.

"You two had better get a room," she teases.

I laugh, then get on with my explanations. I tell Rags about my long-time friendship with Chevelle, our frequent getaways to places other than Hideaway Isle, and how we've been there for each other through thick and thin. I describe the way my last minute trip home came to be, how Chevelle urged me to read the news about Lottie, and how I knew I needed to return to the island to help Grandpa Vern handle the convoluted situation. Once we cover the history, I explain that Chevelle took the liberty of bringing Puck to the airport with her this morning and practically forcing me to eat breakfast with the two of them.

"Is that the difficult news you received?" Rags asks. "The news you mentioned when I found you?"

"It is," I confirm. "It took me by complete surprise."

"You found her?" Chevelle asks. "Where?"

"Hold on, Chev," I say. "I'm getting to that part."

I turn back to Rags, then tell him about my dream of Mom and how Puck and I compared pictures just before he returned home.

"It's her," I proclaim. "My Annie Callaway is Puck's Annie Reed. And apparently, she was Annie Finley before that. I had no idea she was married to anyone before my dad. I definitely didn't know she had another child. No clue."

Rags nods, and I can see the wheels turning in his mind.

"Puck, do you have any relatives still living?" Rags asks.

"I do, sir," he says.

Rags lifts a palm in the air.

"Please, call me Rags."

"Okay, Rags," Puck continues. "And yeah, my father, Herbert Finley."

"So that would be who to Margot?"

Puck stops, then starts again, correcting himself.

"Right. Sorry. I grew up thinking Herbert was my adoptive father. I found out recently that he's actually my biological grandfather. Annie's father."

"That means he's my grandfather, too," I add.

I can hear the mixed emotions in my voice. It's almost unbelievable to think that in a single day on this planet, I lost one grandfather and gained another. How utterly bizarre. Rags can already read my cues. He tilts his head back, appraising me. He knows exactly what I'm thinking.

"That's heavy," he says softly.

"It really is," I reply.

Chevelle nods, but she can tell there's more I need to say.

"Margot, dear," she tries. "Did something happen? Don't forget how well I know you." She leans towards me across the table and lowers her brows. "There's more, isn't there?"

Rags gives my hand a squeeze. He seems to understand that I haven't told Chevelle and Puck about Grandpa Vern. I feel supported by Rags. It's nice. I'm not used to having that kind of backing, but I suppose I'll get used to it soon enough. I have a feeling Rags will be sticking around in my life. I'm not sure how we'll work out the distance, but I imagine we'll figure it out.

I look into Chevelle's eyes and prepare to tell her about Grandpa, but a wave of hurt crashes down on me and I get choked up before I can find the words.

"Would you like me to tell them?" Rags asks.

I nod, relieved.

"Would you?" I ask.

Rags pulls me to him and plants a soft kiss on my forehead. It's perhaps the sweetest gesture ever. I melt into him, incredibly grateful that I have him to lean on.

"I'm happy to," he says, giving my hand another squeeze.

Chevelle looks at him expectantly.

"It's been an interesting day," Rags begins, glancing back and forth between Puck and Chevelle. "Margot and

I met this morning, and quickly realized that we both knew her Grandpa Vern."

"Oh?" Chevelle asks.

"That's my grandfather on my dad's side," I clarify for Puck's benefit. "Vernon Callaway."

"Yeah," Rags continues. "I met Vern when he leased a slot for his boat at my marina. We became friends. We liked to play golf together."

"Liked?" Chevelle asks. "Past tense. You don't play golf together anymore?"

Rags frowns, then continues.

"Margot needed a ride this morning…"

"After she bolted and left us in The Crumby Biscuit," Chevelle says, finishing his sentence.

Rags and I nod, in sync.

"Right," he says. "Margot mentioned that she made a… hasty exit."

He winks at me as he says it, as if we already have private conversations and inside jokes. I suppose we do.

"She was heading to Vern's anyway," Rags continues, "and I thought it would be nice to see him and tell him how uncanny it was that Margot and I met like we did, shortly after her plane landed in South Florida."

"You two sure have hit it off," Chevelle muses.

"Yeah," Puck adds. "I assumed you'd been together a long time."

Rags smiles, and I do, too. We both like the sound of that. It's nice that other people see what we're feeling. There's an ease between us, as if we've known each other forever.

"Nope," I say. "We just met this morning. Crazy, but true."

"I'm just glad we did. That part of today has been outstanding," Rags says.

Chevelle and Puck grin, admiring the dynamic between us.

"Go on," Chevelle says. "You went to Vern's together?"

"We did," Rags replies. "We were there a while, hanging out and talking. It was great. Vern got a kick out of the way Margot and I met. He seemed to approve. But then…"

Rags hesitates, and I think I see him choking up. I'm again touched by his affection for my Grandpa Vern.

"And there was a knock on the door," I say, taking over the storytelling. "Some strange guys were there. Rags and I were in the kitchen getting a snack together. We heard Grandpa say something about not hurting me… or maybe he meant Lottie. He said not to hurt *her*…"

"What?" Chevelle says, concern rising in her voice.

Rags jumps back in.

"We heard a gunshot," he continues. "I'm sorry to say that Grandpa Vern was shot. He's…"

"He's dead," I say. "I can hardly believe it, but my wonderful grandpa is gone."

Chevelle stands and walks behind me, then wraps her arms tightly around my shoulders.

"Margot, I'm so very sorry," she says. "I loved Grandpa Vern, too. He was the best. I can't imagine what you're feeling."

"Thank you," I say, tears threatening to fall once more.

I'm so tired of crying. My head hurts and my eyes are

all puffy. I don't want to do it. Not today, anyway. I need a break to regain more strength.

"I guess that explains the police officer outside," Puck says.

He doesn't say much, but he seems to be following along carefully. I think he's interested in learning about me. I appreciate that.

"Yeah," Rags replies. "The investigator we spoke with earlier assigned an officer to keep watch over Margot. We don't know if she's in danger. Better to take extra precautions than to be careless and have something happen to her."

We all sit silently for a few minutes as the weight of that reality settles in.

"Look," I say, breaking the tension. "I've had a rough day, and I have a lot to deal with come tomorrow. Tonight, I'd love to focus on something positive. Any ideas?"

Puck doesn't hesitate to throw a suggestion out. He must have been thinking about mentioning it.

"We could go to my grandfather's house. He'd love to meet you."

The four of us look at each other, certain that would be something positive. No one wants to push me.

"Do you feel up to it?" Rags asks. "I could put in a call to Tom and ask if his officer has permission to follow us. Assuming that can happen, I think we'd be good to go."

I nod.

"Might as well. Let's do it," I say. "Herbert Finley, I'm coming to meet you."

17

ADDENDUM

There's something about being without any older family members that is unsettling, even to me as an adult in my late twenties. I'm perfectly capable of looking out for myself in the wider world. I've proven that over the past seven years since I fled Hideaway Isle and made a career in the Navy. So, why do I feel so unsteady now?

I've been through the Naval Academy, Officer Training School, Flight School, and a slew of other training programs and exercises that prepared me to make tough decisions and stand firm under pressure, whether that pressure be internal or external. Not only have I taken part in extensive training, but I've excelled in it. I graduated near the top of my class at the Academy, and I master any challenge thrown my way. On top of all that, I handle my own business. I pay my bills. I vote. I donate to charity. I'm a good citizen. I'm even a good samaritan. I stop to help motorists who have flat tires, and I've used my CPR training a time or two when I've found myself on a scene where it's needed.

Sure, I have the money Grandpa Vern gave me when Mom died, but I hardly use it. I'd be fine without it, if I had to be. My everyday expenses are paid by the money I earn. I'm proud of that. I like being self-sufficient and in control of my own life. I suppose it's easy to see why. I couldn't control my parents' death, but by God, I can control having my bills paid on time so that when I lay my head down at night, I know my affairs are in order. No repo man is coming for my car. No eviction notice will ever be taped to the door of my apartment, and no one I encounter in the Navy will ever doubt my professionalism or dedication.

This isn't about money though. There's a feeling I had once. I remember it distinctly. It's the feeling of knowing there are elder family members around to guide you. I miss that desperately. Even when Dad's death rocked me as an elementary school aged child, I had Mom and Grandpa Vern to look up to. I never had to make tough choices without getting their input. I didn't necessarily listen to their advice, but I liked knowing they were available to ask.

Take the college admissions process, for example. I debated which colleges to apply to, and then which major to select. Since I was involved in band and orchestra activities in high school, the admissions process spanned two full years of auditions and campus visits. I had to prepare music to play for auditions based on each college's requirements, and I had to line up a piano accompanist for each one, too. It was a time consuming and complicated process. Mom traveled with me to auditions as far away as North Carolina and Alabama. I never really expected I'd leave the state of Florida for college, but it seemed prudent to cover all the bases. At the time I was auditioning, I didn't know if I'd even get a scholarship offer to any school of music. I suspected I would since I had been selected to participate in Florida's All State Band during three of my high school years. But I didn't know for sure. My strategy was to cast a wide net, hoping that some school would be interested enough to offer me a partial scholarship.

Back then, I didn't know Grandpa Vern had money beyond that of the upper middle class demographic I thought we all belonged in. No one talked to me about money much until the day Mom died and Grandpa Vern sat me down for a frank discussion about his resources. When I was auditioning for music scholarships, I thought I *had* to get them, or else not attend college. Maybe I worked harder thinking that way. I don't know. What I remember, though, is how kind Mom was as we visited schools and I talked through the pros and cons of each with her. She'd sit outside or in the audience while I played my audition piece, depending on the rules at that particular college. Then we'd go to eat somewhere fun nearby and discuss our impressions of the buildings, the professors we met, and how my performance that day compared to others. We had notebooks with charts and checklists, and a big binder that we filled with all the brochures and pamphlets we collected. It was a special time.

Little did I know it would be just a few years until I was thrust into the world on my own, without parents. Thankfully, my phone conversations with Grandpa Vern provided me a little slice of parental guidance, even though I mostly told him what I was doing after the fact rather than asking his opinion before I made a decision. At no point did I stop and consciously think that I no longer had guidance from older, wiser family members available to me. I knew that as long as Grandpa was alive, I did. Just because I didn't ask his opinion before making a decision didn't mean I couldn't decide to do so if I'd wanted to. He probably would have been glad-- honored, even-- to have been asked.

But things have changed now. That's all upended. I suddenly feel like I want to go back and ask Mom and Grandpa Vern a long list of urgent questions. What if they had wisdom that I desperately need, but won't be able to access? What if there is family history I should know? What if I squandered my time with them, not appreciating what I had until it was gone? I kick myself for my immaturity in not realizing Grandpa Vern could leave me, too. I should have known that he could. Of course, he could. Silly me. I suppose I subconsciously clung to the hope that I'd get to keep one older relative for a while. Grandpa was in good shape for his age. I even noted how spry and fit he looked when I saw him this morning. I envisioned him lasting until ninety-five, maybe even one-hundred. He could have been the first Callaway centenarian. Wouldn't that have been grand?

As I think about Puck and his Grandpa Finley, I'm full of mixed emotions. I intend to get a DNA test done so we have undisputable confirmation that Puck and I are siblings, but I already know we are. He looks like Lottie and me. The set of his nose, the roundness of his mouth, and the long, muscular build are the same. I imagine that when I see Herbert Finley, he'll look like Mom, too, which means he'll look like Lottie and me. The family connection will be undeniable, even before any DNA test is administered. I wonder how that will feel. I wonder if I'll become furious at Mom when I hear more about why she abandoned Puck and cut ties with her parents. I also wonder if I'll develop a close relationship with my new grandpa, the one I never knew I had. The thought gives me a twinge of hope and excitement, but it also makes me feel guilty. I don't want to replace Grandpa Vern like a spare part, interchangeable and fluid. Grandpa Vern is-- *was*-- so special to me. I'd never want to hurt his feelings or make him feel less than.

I'm deep in thought as the four of us climb into Rags' Jeep and pull out of his driveway. Chevelle and Puck are situated in the back, despite a lack of legroom. They don't seem to mind. Rags called Tom Marsh, who offered to send a second officer to follow us. That way, one could stay at the house while the other kept tabs on me. It's strange to be the subject of that kind of attention, but I appreciate the fact that Tom is being cautious. I wonder if he's learned any more about the men who shot Grandpa. I'm eager to find out who they are and get to the bottom of this thing with my sister.

"What's on your mind?" Rags asks as he shifts through the gears of his standard transmission as we get up to speed.

"Oh, I'm thinking about so many things," I say. "Grandpa Vern. Lottie. And now Puck and Herbert."

Puck reaches a hand forward and pats me on the shoulder. It surprises me. He's so shy and nervous. It feels nice though. I could get used to the idea of having a big brother. Maybe expanding my circle of people closer to my age can make up for the lack of older relatives, in a way. I can imagine it, although I still can't square up the fact that my new, important relationships are developing on Hideaway Isle when I'm stationed so far away on Whidbey Island. I suppose I have time before I have to make any decisions in that regard. Maybe instead of getting together in other places when Chevelle and I have time off, I'll come home to Florida. Or maybe Chevelle, Rags, and Puck can all meet me. I realize how ridiculous that sounds the instant it crosses my mind. They're all here. Why shouldn't I be, too?

"Anything I can do to help?" Rags asks, placing his hand on my knee once the Jeep is in fifth gear and we're at cruising speed.

I shake my head. "No, but I should try to call Lottie. I dropped a bomb on her earlier when I told her about Grandpa Vern being killed."

"You think she'll answer?" Chevelle asks from the back seat. "That girl is a live wire right now."

"Exactly," I say. "That's precisely what I gleaned from our brief phone call. I have no idea how to handle her. We're such different personalities. And she's hurting. I'm not sure how to get near her without getting myself hurt in the process."

"Like Grandpa Vern," Chevelle adds.

Rags nods. He's protective about Grandpa. I suppose that makes him automatically at odds with Lottie, even though he hasn't met her. A pang of sadness hits me when I consider that. Ideally, I'd want my sister to be close to any man in my life. It stings to realize that her behavior and poor choices may prevent that from happening, no matter how much I'd like it to. At the same time, I don't blame Rags one bit. If Lottie's troubles had any part at all in Grandpa Vern's death, I'm not sure how I'll ever forgive her.

"Yeah," I say, turning things over in my mind.

"Want to call her now?" Rags asks.

The patrol car is following us. It would be a big production to stop somewhere to make a phone call, but it might be too loud to talk in the Jeep.

"You know, I think I do," I say. "Is the road noise usually a problem?"

"Not when we use the vehicle's speaker with Bluetooth. Do you mind?" he asks.

I consider it a moment. I sort of feel like Lottie deserves more privacy, but then again, I'd bet anything that I only get voicemail, anyway. I don't think she has my number, and I doubt she'd pick up a call from an unknown number.

"Sure," I say. "I'll probably just leave a message."

"It isn't far to Herbert's house," Puck adds.

"Okay, I'll make it quick."

We get my phone connected to the Jeep's audio system, then I place the call, carefully dialing the numbers I copied from the handwritten list on Grandpa Vern's wall. The act fills me with anxiety, and a deep sadness. I almost hope Lottie doesn't pick up. I'd like to delay dealing with my sister until another day. It's so much at once.

18

SHOW OF FORCE

W e're parked at Herbert's less than a minute when Rags' phone rings. He glances at the caller ID.

"That's Tom from the police department," he says. "I have to take this."

He pushes the button to connect the call through the audio, the same as he did when I tried Lottie.

"Tom? Hey," Rags says.

Puck and I look at each other awkwardly. I'm sure he told Herbert we were coming. At least, I assume he did.

"Does your grandpa know we're coming?" I whisper to Puck, craning my head towards him in the back seat. "Does he know about... me?"

Puck shakes his head.

"He doesn't?" I say, flabbergasted. "Seriously?"

"He won't mind," Puck replies. "It's fine. He's a nice guy."

Tom's voice booms over the vehicle's speaker.

"Rags, is Margot Callaway still with you?" Tom asks.

"She's right here," Rags replies. "Along with two of her... friends... and the patrol car behind us. What's up?"

"I hate to do this over the phone," Tom says, "but we have some news that you need to hear about right away."

My body stiffens. I can tell it's bad news. I think of Lottie, and fear courses through me. I reach out for Rags' hand. It's there, ready to meet mine.

"Okay," Rags replies. "You're on speaker, Tom. Go ahead."

"Margot, can you hear me?" Tom asks.

I confirm. I wish he'd get on with it and spit it out.

"Yes, I'm here. I hear you loud and clear," I say.

As I wait for Tom to say whatever it is he's working up to, I glance around the property in front of us. It's a beautiful piece of waterfront land, not far from Nimbus Marina. The house is well known by residents and tourists alike. It's one of the nicest ones on the island, right down to the lush landscaping and salt water swimming pool. It's three stories of classic South Florida architecture. I remember Chevelle and I passing it on our bikes when we were kids who were too young to drive. I wonder if Puck grew up in this house. If so, he was probably here when Chevelle and I passed, which makes me wonder if Mom knew he was right here the whole time.

"Margot," Tom says. "There's been an incident."

"Okay? What kind of incident?"

"I'm sorry to be the bearer of bad news, but two officers who were stationed outside of Vernon Callaway's condo were shot and killed this evening. The guys who did it trashed the place, too. They were looking for something."

"Oh, no," Rags says, suddenly scanning our

surroundings like he's been dropped in the middle of a war zone. "Has our escort been informed?" he asks.

"Dispatch is on the line with him as we speak," Tom confirms.

Rags puts the Jeep in reverse and motions for the patrol car behind us to get out of the way. He's ready to bolt, though I don't know where he plans to take us. I suppose it's wise to get out of the open. We're sitting ducks here, the flimsy cover on the Jeep scarcely enough material to keep rain off our heads, let alone protect us from bullets.

In the distance, I see a lantern on the front porch turn on, then the opening of a screen door. An old man steps out, using one hand to block the light from his eyes and the other to wave to us. A feeling of familiarity washes over me as he walks our way and his features come into view. He looks like Mom. A *lot* like Mom. I wasn't prepared for just how much. I've never met the man, but I instantly feel like I've known him all of my life.

"Wait! There's my grandpa," Puck says. "We can't just leave."

"You bet your ass we can," Rags replies, motioning more violently at the cop behind us who is blocking our exit.

"Tom," Rags says, "talk to me. What's the motive?"

"I'm afraid we don't know yet," he replies. "We consider the men armed and dangerous. And we believe Margot and her sisters are potential targets. I'm sending additional officers to your location. Where are you?"

Rags narrows his eyes, thinking hard. I can see him strategizing. I'm practically speechless, taking in the sight of my new grandpa and his beautiful waterfront property while also hearing Tom's words of warning and the terrible news about the police officers who have been killed. Until this very moment, I don't think it hit me just how much danger we're in. I saw Grandpa Vern's lifeless body, but my experiences with death are all accidents. As far as I know, none of my family members have been murdered. No one has chased us down, pursued us. No one has trashed one of our homes looking for something. There hasn't been a bad guy to be mad at, other than God or Fate or Life. This situation is forming up to be very different. Real bad guys are after us for some reason. Our survival depends on finding them before they get to us. I see that now. I'm beginning to think with my Naval Officer head instead of my injured little girl one. Something shifts inside of me. Finally. It's time.

"How should we do this?" I ask Rags.

We lock eyes, and we're instantly on the same page.

"Tom, don't look for us. We'll find you once we know it's safe," Rags says, then he ends the call.

I nod my approval. It's go time.

"Puck and Chevelle, you two need to get out of the Jeep," I instruct. "Right now. I'm sorry, but there's no time to discuss it. Rags and I have to go."

Chevelle nods, giving me a quick hug from the back.

"I'm praying for you, my friend," she says. "Do what you must. I trust the two of you will take care of each other."

I nod, then push her out the door. Puck hangs back, hesitant. Herbert continues to approach us. The old man needs to get inside and take cover. He doesn't realize that danger lurks around us. It hurts my heart to see him so innocent and vulnerable, just like Grandpa Vern was. I want to go to Herbert and tell him we're family. I want to show him pictures of Mom and me, then hug him tightly as we connect over happy memories and connected dots. But I can't. Not yet. I must focus. The danger is real.

"Puck, get your grandpa inside and lock the doors. Get your wife here, too."

"My girlfriend," he mumbles.

"What?"

"She's my girlfriend. We aren't married. She wants to get married…"

"Whatever," I say, cutting him off. "Get Chely here. Keep Chevelle with you. Then stay inside this house until you hear from us. Don't answer the door or the phones unless you know it's someone you trust completely. Even then, don't say anything you wouldn't want overheard."

Rags' mind is working fast, but I can tell he admires my handling of the pressure we've suddenly come under. The feeling is mutual.

"Puck," Rags adds. "What Margot said about not trusting anyone… That includes the police."

"Okay," Puck says, seeming to realize the seriousness. "I'll explain to my grandpa and Chely. I'll keep them safe."

I get the idea my new brother may be rising to the occasion for the first time. It suits him. I'm proud.

"Atta boy," Rags says. "You have a weapon?"

Puck nods. "My grandpa has a few guns."

"Keep them locked and loaded," Rags replies. "Now go. We'll be in touch as soon as we can."

Puck gets out, then opens my door and hugs me tightly. I lean into him. I sure hope that I don't lose the family I've just found. I rather like them.

"Okay," I say after a minute. "Get them inside. See you soon."

Puck nods, then ushers Chevelle and Herbert indoors. I watch the look of confusion spread across Herbert's face as Puck forcefully moves him. Again, it stings to see this man so close, yet I can't meet him. Panic grips me as I fear that I'll never have the chance to hear his voice or look at the fine details of his physical features. I didn't know how much I wanted to do those things, but I long for the chance.

"I know," Rags says. "We'll be back. Hang on."

I nod and grip a handle beside my seat to steady myself as Rags puts the Jeep in four wheel drive and makes his way around the patrol car on our way off the property. The cop in the car looks at us, perplexed. He has his radio against his face, still talking to dispatch. He doesn't seem to know what to do. Apparently deciding to follow us, the guy flips on his lights and sirens, then begins a three point turn to get his car heading in the right direction.

"Damn," Rags says. "We'll have to lose him."

"What about Cap?" I ask. "Can we get him?"

Rags is silent. He's torn.

"It's a risk at this point," he says. "We can't stay at my house. They'll find you there."

"I know," I reply. "But Cap? I think we should go get him."

Rags hesitates again, but finally agrees.

"Okay," he says. "We'll park somewhere out of sight, then go and retrieve him if it looks safe. I love that big guy, but we have to look out for ourselves first. You know that, as hard as it is."

"Good," I say, breathing a sigh of relief. "I'm glad you're willing to try and get him. I wouldn't feel right leaving him behind. He's already made quite an impression on me. Once we get your boy, what then?"

Rags shakes his head. This is a big deal. I now understand the gravity. Whatever these people want, they've now killed cops to get it. That's a huge indication of how ruthless they are. They'll most likely stop at nothing to get what they're looking for. I'm frightened. This is the most harrowing situation I've experienced. I'm on my own out here. I don't have the Navy to provide support like I would if this were a military problem. I can't count on reinforcements or protocols or a stockpile of highly specialized weapons and machinery. By comparison, facing a threat while under the protection of the Navy sounds like a piece of cake.

"I won't let anything happen to you, if that's what you're asking," Rags says.

Tears spring hot to my eyes. I can hardly believe the mess I've found myself in the middle of. The fact that Rags wants to step in the crosshairs with me is touching. It's remarkable, really. He's a truly decent guy. The kind I've been looking for, even though I didn't fully realize it.

"Thank you," I say quietly. "I honestly can't thank you enough."

Rags glances at me as we make our way out onto the road and head south towards his cottage. I'm struck by his grace under pressure. His chiseled features look almost statuesque under the glow from the headlights in front of us. It's as if I've been sent a real-life superhero. A damn sexy one, at that. He cocks his head to one side as he drives.

"Yeah, I hear you," he insists. "And you're welcome. But it's my pleasure. Who knows? Maybe I was born for this."

"Kind of like the old Bon Jovi song," I say with a chuckle. "I was born to be your baby and you were made to be my man."

He smiles broadly.

"Only God would know the reason," he sings, breaking instantly into a full, deep chest voice. "But I'll bet he must have had a plan."

I like the sound of that.

PART III

FATES

TACTICAL

We arrive at Rags' cottage quickly. We consider parking a few blocks away, but hear barking that sounds like Cap's voice and so continue driving.

"Is that him? Or am I imagining things?" I ask as the sound grows louder.

"I think it is," Rags confirms. "And it sounds like he's outside."

We're both uncertain as we approach the house. Rags pulls his Glock from the holster in his belt and holds it down out of sight. I'd meant to mention his gun after the events at Grandpa Vern's earlier, but haven't had a chance. I again wish I'd opted to travel with a weapon. Hopefully, Rags has more than one I can use.

The sound of Cap's barking intensifies the closer we get. I've only known the dog for a day, but I can tell by the tone of his voice that he's sounding an alarm. Something is wrong. Badly wrong.

"Get down," Rags says.

I nod, sliding onto the floor board. I'd prefer to see

what's happening out there, but I get it. I'll follow his instructions. He slows the Jeep to a stop, then whistles one long, shrill tone. I hear paws running madly, then see Rags reach behind him and open the back door for Cap to jump in. The dog sails through the air and into the vehicle as if he's been trained to do exactly that. I reach a hand out to touch Cap, smoothing the fur on one side of his face as he pants to cool himself off. His fur is sopping wet, probably saliva from all the barking.

"Good boy," I say.

"Stay down," Rags tells me.

I feel the Jeep roll forward slowly and make a turn, but it's the opposite direction from his driveway.

"What are we doing?" I ask.

"Shh," he says, raising his gun. "Stay quiet, Margot. Please."

I take a breath and try to settle my nerves. I silently count backwards from one hundred, a little trick I learned after Mom died and I couldn't sleep at night. I'm not sure it will help me now, but I figure it's worth a try. I don't have a better idea. As I move down through the numbers, Rags continues to roll the Jeep slowly, his gun raised. Finally, we make another left turn and begin to pick up speed.

"What did you see?" I ask as he motions the all clear for me to get up.

"Can you handle the full truth?" he asks me.

"What kind of question is that? Yeah, I can handle it."

"I don't mean any offense," Rags says. "I don't want to overwhelm you. I haven't known you very long, and there was the scene at the bench this morning…"

I'm still embarrassed about that. I can't believe that's how Rags and I met. I suppose I shouldn't look the gift horse in the mouth, especially since our chance meeting allowed us the short window of time to chat with Grandpa Vern together before he was killed. But I can understand how Rags is still unsure about my fortitude.

"Yeah, I get that," I say. "But I'm okay. Tell me."

He speeds down the road now, reaching nearly eight five miles per hour on a two lane stretch of highway.

"They'd been there," he says simply. "My front door was wide open and I could see that things were tossed around inside."

"Oh, Rags," I say. "I'm so sorry. Your beautiful cottage…"

"They're just things," he says. "Most of them can be replaced. I'm glad Cap is okay."

"Me, too," I say, scratching the dog under his chin. "I wonder if they were still inside. We haven't been gone long."

I shudder as I think about what a near miss this was. If we'd left the cottage just fifteen minutes later, we probably would have been there when these guys arrived.

"I didn't see any sign of the officer stationed on patrol. The car was there, but it appeared to be empty."

"Damn," I say, shaking my head. "Should we call it in?"

Rags gives me a look. He has already moved on to a contingency plan that I haven't yet realized.

"No. My priority is protecting you."

My eyes widen as I hear this. I'm glad. Tremendously glad, but the implications are startling. Not to mention, I want to ensure the safety of my people: Chevelle, Puck, Herbert. Lottie.

"What do we do next?" I ask. "Should we leave the island?"

"They'll be expecting that. Better to hide in plain sight," he says.

"Okay, but where?"

Before Rags can answer, he slows the Jeep again and pulls into a short driveway that leads to a carport underneath a home that's propped up on stilts. A lot of the homes on the island are built like this to protect the interior from water damage during hurricane season. The storms around here can be brutal. We pull all the way against a concrete wall at the back of the structure and Rags puts the Jeep in park. Two other vehicles are here, a shiny black cargo van and a beaten up Lincoln Towncar that looks like something a retiree on a fixed-income would be driving. I don't ask about them. I'm quickly learning to go with the flow and trust.

"Come on," Rags says. "We're going in."

"Is this where we'll stay? Do other people live here?" I ask.

"I'll explain when we get inside. Hurry, please."

Cap and I follow Rags as he enters the home through a nearby door. Once we're safely inside, he locks a series of chains and deadbolts behind us, then we make our way up a flight of stairs to an open living area.

"Stay put," Rags says. "I'll be right back."

I nod. Cap sits down and leans on my leg. It's apparently his go-to move. It brings me comfort, steadies me. And I need steadying.

I survey the place while I wait. It's not nearly as nice

as Rags' cottage. This living room is small and cramped, and there's a musty smell that seems to be coming from a sectional sofa that's been squeezed in and shoved up against a wall. The painstaking attention to detail at Rags' cottage has been skipped over here. I'm curious about who lives here and why we've come. I'm anxious for a chance to ask Rags questions.

In a few short minutes, he emerges from a bedroom carrying a large black duffel bag. Rags is wearing an additional belt with three kinds of guns attached. I can't tell for sure what they are, but suffice to say he's well-armed. He tosses me a skullcap and a black t-shirt.

"Here, put these on," he says. "We'll do more to disguise your appearance at our next stop, but this is a start."

I do as I'm told without asking questions. I put the new t-shirt over top of my Navy one. It's a few sizes too big, so there's room for both.

Rags goes to a console table near the stairs and reaches underneath until he retrieves a small metal box. He slides it open to check the contents. I get a quick glance and see cash, passports, and a set of keys.

"That'll do it," he says. "Time to move. Let me go downstairs and out the door first. When I give you the signal, bring Cap and join me. We're getting into the Lincoln."

I nod again, paying close attention to every word he says. I don't want to miss anything and cause us trouble. This is too important. I'm convinced my very life depends on us getting somewhere safe and then figuring out how to catch these guys before they do any more damage. That, of course, also means figuring out what they want. I think of Grandpa Vern and the two cops who were killed over whatever this is, and I wonder what happened to the cop stationed outside of Rags' cottage. I don't want any more bloodshed.

Thankfully, the coast is clear when Rags reaches the bottom of the stairs and he signals for Cap and me to join him. Tucking the rest of my long hair under the skull cap, I make my way downstairs and into the Lincoln.

"Stay down again," Rags says, tying a blue bandana around his own head and starting up the engine. "We're going to a houseboat on the other side of the island. I don't want you to be spotted along the way."

"Got it," I say. "Your marina?"

"No, a buddy and I have an arrangement."

"Okay," I reply, desperately wanting to know more.

I force myself to wait patiently for additional explanations. It's tough. I really want to know what in the world prompted Rags to put all of these contingency plans in place. The level of planning he must have done to pull this off is elaborate. We pull out onto the road again and I realize I don't even know where we just were. I'm disoriented. I trust Rags, but it's a little concerning to be so vulnerable. Rags seems to know what I'm thinking.

"It's a lot to take in, yeah?" he asks.

"You can say that again," I reply. "I have lots of questions."

"And I have answers," he replies. "Hang in there until we get settled, then I promise I'll make this make sense."

I nod.

"We won't be on the houseboat long," he says. "We'll spend the night there, but in the morning we'll make a series of vehicle swaps until we get to a safe house where we can stay as long as we need. Don't worry."

I nod again, my eyes wide. There's so much that I can barely begin to process related to what has happened since my plane touched down on Hideaway Isle. At this point, all I can realistically do is go with the flow. I believe Rags is my only hope for getting out of this alive.

I study his facial expressions as he drives. His resolve is strong, the same as his muscular physique. He looks completely at home, changing appearances, evading detection, and moving under the cover of night. I imagine his experience as a Navy SEAL prepared him, but I wonder what made him decide that this kind of threat might one day find him at home in South Florida. Was it a specific concern? Or is this level of readiness consistent with what other former SEALS do? Are there safe houses, weapons, and getaway vehicles hidden in every Navy SEAL's city? Or has Rags taken this further? I want to know.

I feel the crunch of gravel under our tires as the Lincoln slows to a stop. Rags turns off the headlights and it's pitch black outside. We must be in a remote part of the island. If I had to guess, I'd say we're over near the protected wetland nature preserve. There's too much development on the rest of the island to leave anywhere this dark. For the most part, I feel at home in nature, so this suits me.

"Be very careful when you get out," Rags says. "We don't want to use lights, but there are trip hazards. Driftwood, plants… that kind of thing."

"Okay," I say.

"We'll board the houseboat and take it offshore a little

ways before we turn on any lights. It can't move very fast, so slow and steady is the name of the game. We have to blend in. Remember, we want to hide in plain sight. Police cruisers are now stationed by the bridge at Keeper Causeway. They have a roadblock set up and aren't letting anyone on or off the island without permission."

"Wow," I reply. "But okay, I hear you loud and clear. I'm up for this. I promise."

Rags takes my hand and gives it a squeeze, then we step out into the night, the big duffel bag and Cap in tow. It's about a five minute brisk walk from where we leave the car until we reach the houseboat. Rags boards first, checking in every nook and cranny to make sure it's safe. When he gives the signal, Cap and I join him. It's been a while since I've been on a boat, but the familiar sloshing and rocking sensations make me feel at home. We lock the doors and windows tightly, then quietly untether the boat from its dock and drift out to sea.

20

UNWINDING

Rags, Cap, and I spend a quiet night on the houseboat, drifting peacefully not far off the shores of our home on Hideaway Isle. At one point, just before dawn, a Coast Guard vessel slows as it passes by us, but Rags waves and they move on. Apparently, they don't consider us suspicious. We probably look like any other happy young couple, spending a night on the water together in paradise. I blush just thinking about it.

As far as I know, no one is looking for us. The police and Coast Guard activity is centered around the men who killed the cops, who are presumably the same ones who killed Grandpa Vern. Rags has taken us off grid to protect against those killers, not because we've done anything wrong, but because he doesn't trust the police to keep us safe if they can't even keep their own officers alive. I completely understand and agree with him. It's odd being on the run like this though.

It strikes me as ironic that Rags and I are supposed to

be the good soldiers. We pledged our allegiance to our country and to the United States Navy when we signed up for military service. I never expected to find myself having to sneak around and hide like this. Maybe I was naive, but I thought I'd always have the reliable support of the military, the police, and any other official U.S. agency meant to protect citizens. I even thought I'd receive preferential treatment if it came to that since I am an active duty Naval Officer. I'm willing to risk my life in military service. Not once did it occur to me that the other good guys wouldn't be able to protect me if I needed it.

I find myself thrust into a whole new world. Again, it's one that I didn't ask or wish to be a part of. It seems to be a recurring theme in my life. I'd love to break whatever curse has been placed on my family. If only I knew how.

Rags is rooting through his duffel bag as the sun comes up, muttering something about breakfast. We took turns keeping watch overnight. He slept on a futon and left the bed for me, like a gentleman. We didn't talk much. I didn't want to bombard him with the third degree. Besides, I was tired. My nap yesterday only held the exhaustion off for a while. I'll need much more sleep before I get back to any semblance of normalcy. I expect it will take a few solid nights, bare minimum.

The houseboat is nice. *Really* nice. Half of the boat is an enclosed cabin while the other half is an open-air covered deck with a grill, an outdoor shower, and a fully outfitted tiki bar. It isn't a luxury yacht or anything, but it's clean and well appointed. Much better than the beaten up Lincoln we drove here in and the home it was parked underneath. Maybe that's part of the plan. If the various vehicles and safe houses Rags keeps at the ready seem disparate, it might make them harder to connect as being related. Folks who are used to living in the lap of luxury often don't want to slum it. I can tell Rags is comfortable either way. I admire that about him. I suspect we could travel the world together, both able to blend in whether on the crowded streets of a grungy city or the most elegant upscale wineries and restaurants. Being able to go anywhere is an asset, not to mention a tactical advantage. When I have kids, I intend to take them traveling and experiencing different places so they grow up comfortable with all kinds of people and settings. We didn't travel much when I was a child, but I've gotten myself out and about, thanks to the Navy.

I'm still sprawled on the bed, Cap sleeping soundly on my legs. I stretch and look out the window a few feet away. The clear blue water sparkles under the morning sun, as beautiful as ever. Nature is the most predictable thing in my life. It remains constant, changing, but predictably so most of the time. It's far steadier than anything else in my life. And more and more since I arrived back home on Hideaway Isle yesterday morning, I'm remembering how much I love the natural beauty of this island. I smile as I gaze out at the horizon.

"I could get used to this," I say, yawning.

"Oh, yeah?" Rags asks. "Which part? And don't say breakfast in bed because I'm pretty sure all I have in here are MREs."

The military acronym for Meal, Ready to Eat makes my stomach turn just thinking about it. MREs are dried, individual rations for consumption in the field when food preparation facilities aren't available. They are notoriously nasty, although when nothing else is available, they make do. I'd rather choose most any other edible substance.

"Ugh, gross," I say, teasing. "No breakfast burrito by a bench this morning? You're slacking, Bertram."

Rags laughs, the light from the window nearest him highlighting the curve of his muscular shoulders. He's shirtless, wearing cotton shorts tied with a string that dangles artfully at the base of his washboard abs. *How cliché*, I think to myself. Eyeing his athletic torso makes me warm, and pressure builds between my legs. I've been avoiding letting myself get turned on, but in my still-dreary morning state I take in the sight of him and allow myself to fantasize for a moment. I'll bet the covered parts of Rags Bertram are every bit as appealing as the ones I can see. And he's probably a tender lover. A giver. I'll bet he'd take the most exquisite care of me in bed.

It must be obvious that I'm lost in thought because I'm chewing on my bottom lip and staring now.

"Just what are you looking at?" he asks, raising his arms in the air and flexing his biceps like a bodybuilder. "Here for the gun show?"

"You wish!" I reply.

I laugh heartily, placing a hand on my belly and rolling over in bed. Cap groans like an old man when my movements disturb him.

"Oh, hush," I say to the dog.

I *am* here for the gun show, and more. Rags is an interesting combination of competency, humor, and good-natured humility. I'm not sure I've ever met a man like him. I feel completely safe with him and even protected by him, yet he does it in a way that doesn't leave me feeling weak or less than. He respects my autonomy-- admires it even. And he clearly appreciates my intelligence. I'm impressed by what a good fit we seem to be, all the way down to the Navy connection.

"Look at us, Cap," Rags jokes, "competing for the attention of this lovely, badass lady."

Cap groans again, over it. He wants to stay sleeping and we're keeping him from his slumber.

"I think Cap has you beat, by a long shot," I tease back. "After all, he's the one in my bed right now."

"Oh, really? Is that right?" Rags says with a huge grin as he moves slowly towards me.

He winks as he walks, trying to be smooth but looking adorably dorky at the same time.

"See for yourself," I say, waving him on.

"I think I can take Captain America," Rags continues. "He's strong and mighty, but I have the size advantage."

"And now you're touting your large size... in bed... "

Rags throws his head back, jumping onto the bed beside me and tickling my sides. I recoil, full of laughter and a squeal or two. I'm very ticklish. Not to mention, I need some time with nothing but happiness. No family drama, no grief, and no assassins chasing us down. I don't think that's too much to ask. I'm like a steam engine, ready to blow. I need relief, if only for a moment.

"I mean, if the shoe... or whatever... fits..." Rags says, smoothing his hands and placing them low on my hips.

He pulls me against him and I can feel the large swell in his shorts. He wasn't kidding.

His lips are just inches away from mine.

"Yeah?" I ask, moving closer.

"Yeah," he says, pressing my mouth against his with a nibble.

His lips are full and soft. His eyes look even deeper and more enchanting up close. And oh, my God, his touch. It electrifies me. His skin on mine sets off fireworks in places I didn't know could come alive. It feels like we're a matched set, made for one another and realizing it for the first time. It's as if our cells yearn for each other. As if our bodies have waited for this very moment to meet the flesh that will make each of us whole.

I pull back, examining the intricacies of his face.

"What?" he asks. "Too fast?"

I smile.

"Just right," I say. "I'm looking at you because I want to remember this moment."

His expression lights up, and he buries his head in the crook of my neck, kissing my earlobe, my collarbone, and then moving down under the seam on my good ol' Navy t-shirt. *Boy, this t-shirt has been with me for so many life altering memories*, I think. I'll bet this one will be the best yet.

Using one strong hand, Rags explores my body. I moan as he finds his way under my t-shirt and circles my breasts with a soft, yet firm touch.

"Margot, do you have any idea how beautiful you are?" he asks.

I smile, basking in the attention.

"Probably not," I say. "Does anyone?"

He laughs softly.

"You're supposed to say that I'm beautiful, too," he jokes, his mouth and hand still exploring.

I can hardly speak in these conditions, but I try, my voice breathy and incredibly turned on.

"Oh, you are beautiful, alright," I reply. "You are a perfect physical specimen."

"A specimen?" he chuckles. "Like a science experiment, eh? Nice."

He gives my side a little tickle again, and I love the way he brings humor and sex appeal at the same time. It's magical.

"You know what I mean," I say, propping myself up to lean over him. "You're hot. Is that better? *Incredibly* hot. You gave me butterflies the moment I laid eyes on you."

"To be fair," he replies, raising his head up to meet mine and talking between passionate, sultry kisses, "I think you had the butterflies before I ever stepped out of that Mexican restaurant."

I laugh, his mouth still pressed against mine. My round breasts dangle between us, the t-shirt getting in the way. In one smooth motion, I sit up, cross my arms, and pull it off over my head, then toss it onto the floor. While I'm at it, I wrap one leg over him, positioning myself squarely above his bulge.

"Now we're talking," he breathes, his other hand free to explore as well.

We kick Cap off the bed as things heat up. The dog whimpers his protest, but scampers away and settles on the futon.

Rags and I proceed to make sweet, sensitive love, our bodies moving together in a rhythm as ancient as the waves that ripple through the sea below us. When we're finished, we hold each other, hands clasped, as we stare out at the sunshine and stunning scenery, our souls mingling as one. It truly is paradise. My very own paradise. And it's my home. *He* is my home. For the first time in my entire life, I feel so right, so in the flow of what the Universe wants for me. I know for certain this man will be a part of my future. From this moment on, all the rest is history.

21

THE DOTS

As the sun rises high in the sky, Rags and I drag ourselves out of bed. We take our time dressing and getting cleaned up in the outdoor shower. We eye each other, hugging, holding hands, and kissing every chance we get. It's decadent to have the privacy that the houseboat affords. No other human is anywhere in sight. I could stay here forever. In fact, once our troubles are behind us, I might suggest it.

Reluctantly, we make our way back to shore and dock the house boat at a small marina near a campground. It's a gorgeous day, like most here on our little island. I'm still surprised at how relaxed and at home I feel here now. In fact, I wish I'd come home sooner. If I'd known Rags was waiting for me, I would have.

The sound of laid-back beach music wafts through the pines that line the campground. As we get closer, I hear that it's *Island Song* by Zac Brown Band. Zac and his guys sing about passing them a beer, singing along, and losing track of your timing down in the islands. It's the perfect backdrop for a lazy summer day. I have to remind myself that we're hiding from whoever killed Grandpa Vern and those cops. It's tempting to want to join the people playing the music for a leisurely afternoon. I am on leave from my job, after all.

"Sounds like a party," Rags says as we step off the boat and onto a dock with wooden planks. "I might like to hang out a while, under different circumstances."

"I was just thinking the same," I reply. "I'm on leave, and love all the rest and relaxation I can get."

Rags winks at me and leans over to plant a warm kiss on my neck.

"Patience, little one. I think there will be plenty of time for that yet."

I chuckle.

"What's with calling me little one?" I ask.

"Didn't Vern call you Little M?"

"Yeah, but…"

"So, I'm using a modified version. Is that okay with you? I mean, you are little compared to me, anyway. You have the tiniest waist. And pretty, delicate features, even though you're taller than most women. Oh, and you're strong though. Don't get me wrong..."

"You're overthinking this," I say, laughing. "Grandpa Vern did call me that. I suppose you can modify it for your own use if you really want to."

Rags smiles, attaching a leash to Cap's collar, then hoisting the duffle bag over his shoulder.

"Good," he says. "Done. You can call me anything you want. Just don't call me late for dinner."

This guy. Rags is hilarious in a dorky way. And oh, so lovable. I swat him on the shoulder, and he pretends to be injured. Cap watches, gazing up at us affectionately. I must say, the three of us make quite the nice little family.

"Where to next?" I ask, once I can do so with a straight face.

"Oh, right," Rags says. "You distracted me earlier and I didn't have a chance to share details of my plan."

I roll my eyes.

"Mm hmm," I say. "I'm not sure who distracted who, but go on."

He smiles. I don't think a smile has left either of our faces for hours now.

"I have a Subaru wagon waiting for us in the parking lot…"

"I have a Subaru," I add enthusiastically.

"Yeah?"

"Back in Washington State. I just bought it recently. My first automobile purchase as an adult. I must admit, I'm pretty proud of it."

"Alright," Rags says. "I guess I can see you being a Subaru girl, all safe and outdoorsy, especially up in the mountains of the Pacific Northwest."

It occurs to me just how much Rags and I still have to learn about each other. I wish we had time to focus on nothing but that. I look forward to hearing about his childhood, his time as a Navy SEAL, his likes and dislikes. I want to know it all. To take it in and integrate it with who I am so that together we make a stronger, more perfect union. My mind practically hums thinking about it all.

"I'll probably feel right at home in yours then," I say.

Rags continues.

"We'll drive that to the safe house where I intend for

us to stay until the mystery of who killed Vern is solved and I'm certain the coast is clear. I won't allow you to be in any danger, Margot. I'd never be able to live with myself if something happened to you."

He stops to brush a strand of hair behind my ear. I've let my locks flow freely now, in all their twisty glory. Rags seems to like them that way. He keeps reaching out to touch and stroke my curls.

"What's this campground called?" I ask. "I don't think I've ever been here."

"Hideaway Park. It's a cozy spot. It's filled mostly with locals who want to avoid the tourists, but some out-of-towners find the place, too. The square where cruise ships pull up and dock is just around that corner, less than a mile away," he explains, pointing.

I nod. I never really lived on Hideaway Isle as an adult. I'm sure there are nooks and crannies that I wasn't introduced to as a child. I intend to ask Rags a lot of questions once we're settled in at the new place. Hopefully, the safe house is nice like his cottage and the houseboat. Although, I'm okay with lower end accommodations if that's what we have to work with. I'm truly not picky.

"The parking lot is just past the row of picnic tables in the distance," Rags explains. "The Subaru should be there towards the back of the lot. It's silver. A newer model."

"You own these things?" I ask. "The cars, the houses? The houseboat?"

"I do."

I shrug my shoulders, making a mental note to learn how Rags came into enough money for all of this. Maybe it's from the success of Nimbus Marina. Chevelle once mentioned that the new owner had turned it around since taking over a few years ago. But I wonder if Rags comes from a wealthy family. He mentioned being from the Charleston, South Carolina area. I'd love to visit. To meet his parents.

Rags holds my hand as we walk. I take Cap's leash from him, wishing to help out since he's carrying the big duffle bag. I doubt Cap needs a leash though. He's such an exceptional, intelligent animal. I suspect the leash is more for other people's benefit. It probably makes them feel better to see a leashed dog with an owner who is following city leash laws. Not every dog is as well behaved as Cap, and the general public can't necessarily tell how good he is at first glance. I find that I'm proud for the chance to lead Cap as the three of us walk together. It's an honor to be with a creature like him.

A smattering of people come into view as we near the campground. They're milling about. One crowd of six or seven has folding chairs set up in a circle. A few others are setting up a tent on a grassy section of land.

"How do you want me to act around these people?" I ask, remembering Rags' insistence that I stay down as we drove last night.

"Just act natural," he says while we walk through the congested area. "Hide in plain sight."

I nod, keeping my gaze fixed ahead. A little boy comes up to pet Cap. He's probably nine or ten.

"I like your dog," he says cheerfully.

I smile and pause politely. Cap enjoys the interaction, showing his pearly whites and thumping one leg when the boy hits the right spot on the dog's back. After a moment,

Rags tugs gently on my hand. I excuse us, and we continue on through the small crowd.

Being around these people makes me nervous. I tell myself to keep it together. If I act nervous, that will cause them to notice us, for sure. Better to blend in.

"Relax," Rags whispers.

"I'm trying."

By the time we're roughly halfway to the parking lot, I finally do relax. Rags points out the silver Subaru. Seeing it there waiting for us and knowing we're close eases my mind. We can make it. Rags squeezes my hand. Now for a quick car ride-- nothing is very far away on the island-- and we'll be at the safe house where no one can find us. We'll have plenty of time while there to strategize, sort things out, and help police capture Grandpa Vern's killer. I'll have to tend to Grandpa's affairs, of course. There will need to be a memorial service, and I'll have to clean out and sell his condo. But then Rags and I can have a little fun before I have to go back to Whidbey Island.

I skip over thoughts of my sister and her predicament-- the tour boat accident, her recklessness. I want to find and help her, but there's a lot to do first. I'm beginning to get angry with Lottie for her part in all of this. My feelings about my sister seem to swing from one extreme to the other over the past few days, depending on my mood. If I knew more, I'd be better equipped to make judgments. I push those concerns away in favor of putting one foot in front of the other and getting to the safe house without being recognized.

As we make our way along the final stretch towards the car, I notice one last couple we must pass. Thankfully, they appear to be too wrapped up in each other to notice us. A pair of young women, both with long blonde hair, deep tans, and skimpy bikinis, are entangled together in a hammock, pawing at each other and making out. They have the hammock strung between two pine trees and a speaker positioned nearby. The Zac Brown Band music is coming from them. I smile as I think about canoodling with Rags in the houseboat earlier. Love is grand, and this settling is perfect for those feelings to blossom.

I smile at Rags, gesturing towards the ladies.

"We're not the only ones with that idea," I say quietly. He raises his brows.

"I see. I'll cuddle up in a hammock with you any time you want," he replies. "We should make a to-do list."

I laugh, leaning into Rags as I walk. I glance back at the young women. I don't mean to invade their privacy. It's just that I'm drawn to them for some reason, compelled to look at them. They're probably about Lottie's age. They remind me of my sister. Especially the one with the longest, whitest blonde hair. If I didn't know better, I'd think she actually was Lottie. The set of her nose, the angle of her shoulders. She's thinner than Lottie, but...

Oh, my God.

I suddenly drop Rags' hand and Cap's leash, my limbs rendered useless. My knees buckle and I stumble, my mouth hanging open. Rags catches me by the forearm and steadies me. Otherwise, I'd be on my knees on the sandy ground.

"Lottie?"

It's her. I see it clearly now. And I kick myself for taking so long to recognize my own sister. I've been staring at her for several long minutes. She looks up at me, her lips still pressed against her partner's, her hands all over the other woman's body as they grab and grope hungrily.

"Margot?" she says, lifting her head up like a meerkat, a look of confusion on her face.

Rags studies my face, quickly coming up to speed. He picks up Cap's leash, then puts an arm around me to hold me upright and let me know he's here for emotional support. He doesn't seem concerned that I've been recognized. I suppose Lottie isn't a threat. Not directly.

"I… um…" I stammer. "What are you doing here?"

I glance at her girlfriend or hookup or whatever.

Lottie swings her legs over the side of the hammock, sitting upright.

"This is Basia," Lottie says. "Basia Guthrie."

I nod and force myself to smile.

"Basia," Lottie continues, "this is my sister, Margot."

Basia throws herself upward, standing behind the hammock. She wipes the saliva off her lips as if I'm a parent who has just caught her child in an uncompromising position. I don't like the feeling. I'm no parent, and Lottie is no longer a child. It's long past time she takes responsibility for herself as an adult.

"Your what?" Basia asks. "You never told me you had a sister."

22

REUNITED

I'm still gawking, a dumbfounded expression on my face when Rags brings me back to the situation at hand. He leans close to my ear and whispers.

"Margot, we have to keep moving. Do you want to bring your sister and her friend with us?"

I look at him, perplexed.

"Is that an option?"

He nods.

"I don't mind bringing them along. It's up to you," he confirms.

Lottie sits straighter in the hammock, putting her hands on her hips.

"Who is this poser? And what is he talking about?" she asks.

Her insult burns. I know she's looking for a reaction, but I don't want her disrespecting Rags, even a little. Heat rushes to my face and I can feel myself turning red.

"I'm Rags Bertram," he says, reaching to shake her hand. "Pleased to meet you, Lottie. And you, Basia."

Ever the gentleman, even when dealing with a spoiled brat. I don't deserve this man. I'm not sure I'd be so kind if I were in his shoes. Lottie's belligerent attitude comes across loud and clear. She thinks she knows better than everyone else. It's not attractive. I wonder what Basia sees in her, beyond the physical. I'd like to believe there's more to their relationship than that. I'm not so sure.

"Lottie," I say, hoping to reason with my sister. "I left you a voicemail. And you heard what I said on the phone about Grandpa Vern, right?"

I don't reach for her. I don't feel like hugging my sister right now. Maybe not ever. She doesn't reach for me either. We're several feet apart, two sentries on guard.

"Yeah, so?" she replies.

"Aren't you sad about Grandpa?" I ask. "It was horrible… they just shot him in cold blood…"

She narrows her eyes and I think perhaps she's trying to choke back her emotions. I can't tell, though. It's possible she doesn't care. I wonder if she's drunk or on drugs. I wouldn't be surprised at this point. I know she loved Grandpa. I'm just not certain she's in touch with reality to properly grieve him now.

"What do you want with me?" she asks, her tone cold.

Basia takes a step closer to Lottie and places her hands on her shoulders. I can't tell if she's sympathetic to what I'm saying or not. It might help if Basia is on our side, so I decide to appeal to her, too.

"Basia, Lottie, we need to talk to you both, to be sure you're not in danger," I explain. "Even better if the four of us can put our heads together and figure out who killed Grandpa Vern. Would you mind coming with us? To lunch maybe? So we can talk."

Rags shoots me a look and I remember the MREs. I look back, to communicate that I had to offer something other than a blindfolded ride to a safe house. Surely, he gets that.

"Okay, yeah," he says. "I can drop you three off and then go pick up some takeout."

Lottie raises her head to look back at Basia. They're considering it.

"I don't know…" Lottie mumbles.

My pulse quickens and I feel the heat intensifying on my face. We need to talk to Lottie. She probably has information that will be key to figuring all of this out. If she won't cooperate and work with us, it will make things exponentially more difficult. Not to mention, something could easily happen to her with the killers on the loose. I suddenly feel like it's now or never. This is my chance to set things right and reconnect with my little sister. If I can't-- or don't-- I might never see her again. The probable descent into darkness if we part ways here is too harrowing to allow. I have to change the course of this thing. And quick.

"We have a brother," I blurt.

Rags looks surprised, but keeps his arm snug around me.

"What?" Lottie asks, her face balling up.

"His name is Puck. He looks like us, Lottie. He's older. In his thirties. He knew his mom was named Annie, and we compared pictures. His Annie is our Annie. I know it sounds crazy, but it's true."

A single tear falls from my sister's eye. She wipes it away quickly, but I think I might have finally gotten to her.

"That's impossible," she says, although I note a glimmer of recognition in her eyes.

I wonder if she somehow knew. Did Puck approach Lottie first? There's a lot I might have missed, given that I'm the only one who lives on the other side of the country. I decide to move on without asking if she knew. I don't want to antagonize her.

"I thought the same thing at first, but after talking to Puck and seeing the pictures, I'm sure." I proceed cautiously, well aware how precarious the situation is. "He'd like to meet you. And… we have another grandfather, too. Annie's father is still alive."

Basia appears sympathetic. Thank God. She nudges Lottie from behind. Lottie doesn't look back, but she clearly feels the prod. After a long few minutes of silence, Lottie speaks.

"I suppose lunch wouldn't hurt anybody," she says warily. "The dog's coming?"

"He is."

I pump my fist in the air before I can stop myself, and I think I see a slight smile on Lottie's face. I quickly regret it and tone things down. I don't want to appear too eager. Rags smiles, too, and I begin to get excited. I'd love to somehow establish a better rapport with my sister. After everything that has taken place recently, I hate to say it, but we need each other. And now me with Rags and her with Basia, and us with Puck and Herbert, plus Chevelle and Puck's girlfriend and their baby. We have the makings of a great group, if only we can get over ourselves and work together for the greater good.

"That will be nice," I say in as neutral a tone as I can muster.

"We're in an RV," Lottie says. "Do you have a place we can park it near your house?"

"My car is here," Rags says, gesturing towards the Subaru. "The silver one right over there. You two can ride with us. I'll bring you back here when you're ready."

Lottie looks at Basia, who nods her agreement. Rags doesn't mention anything about us being in hiding or his place being a safe house. I follow his lead and go along with it. I don't want to spook these young ladies. That's the last thing we need right now. It's imperative that we keep this casual and low key.

"Okay," Lottie agrees. "As long you as you promise to bring us back the minute we want to leave."

"Done," Rags says, and I can tell my sister believes him.

Rags has an air of dependability about him. He's too upstanding, too noble to lie. What you see with Rags Bertram is what you get. I'm glad. I prefer it that way. In fact, I've yearned for that kind of unabashed honesty in my life. I'm much that way, and without even realizing it, I've wanted someone who shares my values and meets my level of integrity. That's the kind of foundation that a solid relationship can be built on.

When it comes to my sister, on the other hand, I'm not sure I can trust her as far as I can throw her. We'll see. I fear she'll push her luck. One step at a time.

Lottie and Basia go back to their RV and change into shorts and t-shirts, then the four of us pile into Rags' silver Subaru. Cap sits in the back seat between Lottie and Basia. As we ride, we chat cordially about the summer heat and how there seem to be more and more tourists coming to our island every summer. It's interesting, because the weather is nicer in the winter months, yet Hideaway Isle now sees the biggest crowds in summer. Lottie mentions that it's probably because kids are out of school and families have time for vacations over summer break. I suspect she's right. Rags mentions noticing an uptick in summer visitors after Hideaway Isle became a regular stop for cruise ships last year. All the major cruise lines now come to our little island on their way further south into the Caribbean when there isn't room to dock in Key West. We've alleviated the congestion there and afforded passengers an additional destination on their way to places like Cozumel and Cancun, the Cayman Islands, Turks and Caicos Islands, and the Virgin Islands. It's good for our little island's economy, so we can't complain.

"Do you work directly with tourists?" Lottie asks Rags.

Her tone towards him has softened. Maybe she thinks he'll be sympathetic about her situation with the boat tour accident and the angry people who claim she was negligent. I'd like to hear more of that story, so I stay quiet and let her and Rags talk. Lottie might feel more comfortable talking to him than me, anyway. There's so much baggage between us. I trust Rags to be sensitive to that baggage, even though he doesn't know all of it yet. He knows enough to get the idea.

"I actually do," he replies. "I own Nimbus Marina. Have you heard of it?"

He knows they have. It's the largest and most prominent marina on Hideaway Isle. Everyone has heard of it.

"Yeah, nice," Lottie says. "So, you know what a pain in the ass it can be to work with the public. They're so bitchy sometimes. And needy. It sucks the life right out of you."

I cringe. Someone involved in the death of fifteen people who trusted their safety to your company should not be talking like that. Now I see exactly what Grandpa Vern meant when he said Lottie is saying all the wrong things. *Aye yai yai.* Rags handles my sister's immaturity in stride.

"It can be frustrating," he confirms. "I don't mind, though. I look at it as an opportunity. When someone chooses to do business with me, I know they've considered their options and decided they can trust me. I do my best to make sure my team and I live up to their expectations."

Nailed it. Rags affirmed her feelings, but flipped the negative into positive. An opportunity is right. *Way to go, Rags.* Lottie nods, the shift in her thinking immediately obvious, as if she hasn't ever thought about it that way. Surely, someone has said it that way to her. Rags couldn't have been the first, could he? Either way, I'm encouraged.

"Yeah, maybe," Lottie says, staring out the window.

She doesn't mention her company and what happened. I suspect that may be why she's hiding out in an RV.

"Hey, Lottie," I begin, turning the focus back to the men who are after us. I want to find out if they've been to her place, too. "Where are you living now?"

She jerks her head toward me, immediately defensive.

"What is it to you?" she asks in a nasty tone.

"I'm not trying to pry," I say. "I ask because someone

broke into Rags' cottage, where I was staying. Also, they went back to Grandpa Vern's condo last night and killed the two cops stationed outside. They trashed both places. We think they're looking for something."

Rags nods agreeably, confirming my story.

I see Basia shoot Lottie a look across the back seat. There's something to be said, and she wants Lottie to do it.

"I haven't been home in a while," Lottie says.

"I wonder if these guys have been to your place, too," I muse.

Basia opens her eyes wide and gestures with her head for Lottie to give us more details.

"I've sort of been staying more off the radar… after what happened…"

I smile sympathetically. At least, I hope it comes across that way. It's hard to resist the urge to scold my little sister and ask what the hell she was thinking. I assume she's talking about the boat tour accident.

"Grandpa Vern told me about the accident," I say softly. "It's why I came back to visit. I wanted to help."

Lottie rares up in her seat, angry.

"Help?" she asks. "Oh, that's choice, Margot. You want to help."

She laughs in a whiny, fake voice that sends chills down my spine. It almost sounds manic, and I wonder if my sister is mentally ill. Her anger seems extreme. She's unstable. Maybe she's just that way with me. I oscillate between wanting to choke her and feeling like I should cut her some slack after everything she's been through, give her a break.

"I did. I'm sorry I haven't been back to visit in so

long," I say earnestly. "I should have come home more often."

Rags nods and winks discreetly. His support means so much.

"You shouldn't have left me in the first place!" Lottie shouts. "Damn you, Margot. I was a kid. I counted on you. And you just... disappeared. How am I supposed to feel about you?"

I'm surprised by how blunt she's being. I expected her pain to be hidden more deeply, harder to tap into. But, no. It's on the surface, real and raw. It brings my pain to the surface in response. Perhaps that's why I stayed away. My sister's pain intensified my own. As long as she's around, I can't push it down and pretend I'm okay. As long as she's around, there's no way out. Only through.

"That's fair," I say.

I want to say more, but it's hard. I'm not prepared. Even though I came home to deal with Lottie and her issues, I didn't expect to be called out within the first fifteen minutes of seeing her face to face. I didn't realize that the most prominent point in her mind was that I'd left her. I was essentially a child when Mom died, too. Nineteen is hardly an adult. I did the best I could. I had to leave to save myself.

Rags picks up on my distress and steps in.

"We're almost there," he says.

"To the house that was broken into?" Lottie asks.

It's a reasonable question. At least, she's tracking.

"No," Rags says. "We're staying off the radar today in the hopes that those guys don't find us. The house we're going to now is a vacation rental property I own. It's nice. You'll like it. There's plenty of room for everyone."

Lottie accepts his explanation and doesn't ask any more questions. Basia remains silent. I hope she'll warm up soon. I don't want her to feel uncomfortable, though I might be silent, too, in her shoes.

"Sounds good to me," I say, glad for a chance to change the subject.

23

OVER HERE

Rags points as we round a corner and approach a darling little cottage that looks a lot like the home he lives in. This one is a pale blue with a wooden door stained the color of honey. No shutters. The roof rises to an A-line above a covered front porch. The landscaping is impeccable, just like at Rags' primary residence. A decorative sign by the front door reads *Heron Cottage* in script letters

"Nice place, Bertram," I say, stepping out of the car for a better view. "Did you name it?"

Rags nods proudly.

"I did," he replies. "There's a great white heron that hangs out in the backyard from time to time. Gorgeous. The name seemed to fit."

All three of us ooh and ah over the property as Rags soaks in our compliments.

"You rent this place out to vacationers?" I ask.

"Yep," he confirms.

As I walk towards the house, I can tell the lot is deep,

meaning the house is significantly bigger than it appears from the front. Drawn by the long driveway and the faint scent of what I suspect is a salt water swimming pool, I make my way to the backyard. Sure enough, there's a rectangular pool with just as much lush, pretty landscaping around it as is around the front porch. I can smell the salt. A screened porch on the back looks cozy.

"What are you, some kind of house flipper? Or an architect or something?" I ask my guy. "I didn't get a good look at the one on stilts, but your other two properties are amazing. Dreamy, even. I think I like this one better than the first."

Rags leans down to kiss me.

"I'm definitely not an architect. A house flipper, maybe. The one on stilts belongs to a buddy who doesn't have my penchant for home and garden design," he tells me between kisses.

This makes complete sense.

"You can take your pick," he continues. "Or I can fix one up just for you. I'll have to do something to pass the time when you go back to Whidbey Island."

I smile, but the thought of leaving Rags pierces my heart like a dagger. The fact that he's thinking about it too makes it all the more painful. This man is doting on me, which leads me to wonder why the cottage is empty right now. It's too gorgeous to go unrented if it were made available.

"Wait," I say, stopping where I am. "Rental properties are usually occupied this time of year. Did you kick people out so we could get in here?"

He shrugs. "What if I did?"

I shake my head.

"Wow," I say. "I feel kind of bad about that."

He scoops me up in his arms and pulls me in close.

"Don't you know by now?" he asks. "I'd do anything for you, Margot Callaway. Your happiness means more to me than I can adequately express with words. But you'll see it in my actions. Every single day. I promise you."

I blush, I'm so touched. I've never been treated so very nicely, yet I've always wanted to be. I imagine Rags would treat our kids just as well. The thought makes my heart flutter. I no longer stop myself from picturing a future with Rags. Marriage, kids, the works. I can't fight the feelings I'm having. And why should I? He's everything I could ever ask for in a life partner. Like Grandpa Vern said, I should let it happen. Rags seems to feel the same way.

"You're too good to me," I say.

"Yeah, I *was* good this morning," he teases, smacking me on the backside. "I didn't hear any complaints. Quite the contrary."

Rags and I seem to fall naturally into a pattern of easy banter and affection. I nearly forget the young ladies are here once we start up. I do remember, though, and I turn my attention back to them. They're holding hands and gazing into each other's eyes, apparently inspired by the attractive surroundings and the chemistry that Rags and I can't seem to hide. It does my heart good to see my sister smiling. She deserves to find happiness, that's for sure. If Basia makes Lottie happy, then I'm a supporter. I don't know anything about Basia yet, but I suppose I don't need to. If she sticks around, I'll learn plenty in time. She seems bright. Most importantly, she seems to like Lottie.

Rags leads us inside as Cap follows dutifully behind, wagging his tail. We walk past the pool and enter through the back porch. I'm awestruck by how nice everything is. I can't get over it, but I consciously focus on enjoying the present moment instead of questioning things. I'm just glad I don't have to duck down and hide like I did last night. Rags thinks we're safe here. I trust him.

The interior of Heron Cottage is every bit as nice as the outside. Again, I'm impressed by the attention to detail in every room. Cap plops down on a blue and white rug in front of the beige living room sofa, clearly feeling at home. I start to mention the beige sofa and how it's similar to the one I recently purchased for my apartment, but decide I'll save that topic for another time. I prefer to stay mostly quiet so that I can remain alert and attentive to our guests. I do love how Rags and I seem to share the same taste in homes and furniture, though.

"Make yourselves comfortable," he says. "I'll go get some takeout, as promised. Do burgers and fries sound okay? I know a place a few blocks from here."

"Monty's Burgers and Fries?" Basia asks.

"That's the one," Rags confirms. "Sound good?"

We agree, all for burgers. Rags makes a Jimmy Buffet reference to cheeseburgers in paradise being heaven on earth with an onion slice. We all laugh, entertained. We discuss the menu and tell Rags our orders, which he remembers without writing them down, like a waiter at a fancy restaurant. I chuckle, wondering if there's anything he can't do. When he has the specifics memorized and he's about to walk out the front door, Lottie stops him. I hold my breath, wondering if she's going to say that she wants to leave.

"Um, if you don't mind," she begins sheepishly, "I live near here, in a condo. Would you stop by to see if the place has been touched?"

Lottie thrusts her hand towards Rags, a silver key in her open palm.

"Not at all," he replies. "Happy to do it."

She appears relieved. Her shoulders relax, and I can see the worry leave her face. I relax, too. Perhaps she's beginning to loosen up and trust us. Or to trust Rags, at least.

I marvel at my sister's choice to live in a condo instead of a house. It's a logical pick, I suppose. Lottie lived in Grandpa Vern's condo with him for her middle and high school years. The setup must feel like home. So, I take it she didn't spend all of the million dollars Grandpa gave her on the boat tour company. I'm glad. I can also assume that she has enough sense to stay away from her place right now. Maybe she's savvier than I give her credit for.

"The building is on the Corner of Main Street and Fishery Road," Lottie adds. "My condo is on the fourth floor, which is the top. Zoning regulations around here don't allow anything higher. My unit is number 421."

"Got it," Rags confirms.

She thanks him, then sort of skips off to join Basia on the sofa. They have their phones out and begin taking selfies together, my sister grinning and leaning her cheek close against Basia's. Lottie seems like such a girl in this moment. Such a child. I suddenly feel protective of her. I was almost exactly the age Lottie is now when Mom died. I wasn't ready to be on my own. Neither is she. Not completely. I'd like to be a source of moral support and guidance for my little sister. If she'd let me. That remains to be seen.

Rags leans in to kiss me goodbye.

"Hey," he whispers as he pulls back. "Why don't we invite the others over? Maybe putting heads together and getting everything out in the open is the most expeditious way to go."

"The others?"

"Puck, Chevelle... and Herbert."

I agree, promising to make the calls and gather everyone together. I'm thrilled at the prospect of uniting whatever family I have left. I didn't realize the thought of it would please me, but it does. It really does.

"Good," Rags says. "Lock the doors and don't open them for strangers. Okay?"

I nod.

"Seriously, Margot," he presses. "I don't mean to sound alarmist and I don't expect trouble here, but you never know. Be careful."

I stare into Rags' eyes, looking for any hint that he knows more than he's telling me. Except, of course, he knows more than he's telling me. We haven't had that heart-to-heart talk. There's so much I'm not yet privy to. It isn't because he's trying to keep things from me or coddle me. We simply haven't had the chance.

"Is there anything I should know?" I ask.

He sighs, thinking.

"Just that these guys are ruthless. I suspect they'll stop at nothing to get whatever it is they're after. They don't care about any of us. We're just impediments in their path. Most likely, the killers are hired guns. They probably don't even have the authority to make judgments. Someone higher is calling the shots."

I nod, my body tightening with apprehension. It's terrifying to think about. Rags puts a strong hand on my shoulder, steadying me.

"We'll get through this," he confirms, then kisses me on the cheek. "Door locked. No strangers. I'm going to let Cap ride along with me. We'll be back before you know it."

I kiss him back, meeting his lips with my own. We linger for a moment and I can't help but feel like everything will turn out okay. We'll somehow figure out who's behind this mess. We'll turn them in to Tom at the police department. Then we'll move on with our lives. For the first time in my life, I see a future for more than just myself. I want that future. I'm willing to fight for it.

I gather my strength and assure Rags that I can handle a short while here without him. I know he wouldn't leave me if he thought I couldn't do it. I close and lock the front door behind him, glancing suspiciously at the street out front. All is quiet. Not another person in sight.

"Doors are locked. We're good," I say as I reenter the room with Lottie and Basia.

"What are you? Paranoid or something?" Lottie asks.

There's that animosity again. It's never far from the surface when she's talking to me. I smile and ignore her question, doing my best to let Lottie's nasty attitude roll right off. Like water off a duck's back, as Mom used to say. Little did she know it would be my own little sister hurling the insults.

I sit down with my phone in hand and text Chevelle.

. . .

Long story, but we found Lottie.
  Can you bring Puck and Herbert and come over for a talk?

A CONVERSATION BUBBLE SHOWS UP IMMEDIATELY. CHEV must have been waiting by the phone. She's such a good friend. I know she's been worried about me.

I'm with Puck at the Finley house now.
  Give me an address and twenty minutes. Be right there.

I PULL THE PHONE TO MY CHEST, COVERING MY HEART. I knew I could count on her. Butterflies fill my stomach. This will be one of the biggest, most important days of my life. I think about Mom and wish she were here to help explain. Then I remember the dream and what she said about being sorry. Whatever she did or didn't do, it's up to those of us who are left to make the best of it. I've been alive long enough to see that sometimes even the worst mistakes bring good things that wouldn't have come to pass otherwise. We can make good out of this. I know we can.

24

SISTERS

"What are you grinning at?" Lottie asks, noticing my mood.

"I was texting with my friend, Chevelle. You remember Chevelle, right, Lottie?"

"Yeah. So?"

"So, she's with our brother, Puck, right now," I explain. "Rags and I thought it might be nice to have them come over, if that's okay with you."

Lottie shrugs. "Sure."

I'm surprised. That was easier than I expected. I seriously wonder if she somehow knew about Puck before I did.

"Lottie," I try, "you didn't seem shocked to learn about Puck. Did you know about him already? Before I mentioned it?"

Lottie glances at Basia, who nods her on. The two of them go back and forth, Lottie apparently hesitant to share with me. She takes a long, deep breath.

"Mom told me about him."

"What do you mean?" I ask. "She told you before she died? You *knew*?"

Lottie hems and haws, trying to make what she's saying sound reasonable. She can't. Because it doesn't.

"You won't believe me if I tell you," she says, pouting.

"Try me," I reply.

She shakes her head, twirling a section of her long blonde hair absentmindedly.

"Fine," she blurts. "Mom told me in a dream. She comes to me."

I swallow hard, remembering my own dream of Mom during my nap yesterday. It seemed so real. I can't help but wonder if she really is communicating with us. If she is, I wonder if Puck dreams of her, too.

"Okay," I say. "I heard something about that."

"From who?" Lottie asked, her voice rising.

"Grandpa Vern told me."

My sister appears to be upset by this revelation, but at the same time, her face softens. Maybe the mere mention of Grandpa's name is getting to her.

"He did, huh?" she asks. "I didn't know you two talked about me like that."

It's like I'm walking on eggshells. One false step or one statement that strikes Lottie wrong, and she'll clam up, shutting me out. I hate being in this position. I guess I deserve it. I left my sister behind. She reminds me every few minutes how angry she still feels. But I wonder what it will take for her to consider my experience. I wish she could understand how hard it was for me to leave Florida and join the Navy. I cried so hard, so many nights. There wasn't a rulebook. I made my way the best I knew how. And now I've apologized for leaving. It suddenly feels like my apologies may never be enough.

"Grandpa knew I cared for you and wanted to be sure you were okay," I say softly. "I guess he thought I'd want to know that Mom showed up in your dreams. I miss her. Terribly."

Basia looks hard at Lottie again, prompting her. To my surprise, Lottie throws her hands in the air dramatically. I startle, my nerves just about shot after the last few days. My sister is volatile. The only thing about her behavior I can predict is that it will be unpredictable. I wonder how long Basia has been in the picture and how she stands Lottie's erratic nature.

"Fine," Lottie says to Basia. "I'll tell her."

My eyes widen as I look at my sister expectantly.

"Basia is psychic," Lottie says. "She has premonitions. She's had them since she was a kid."

Basia nods to confirm.

"I can't help it," she says.

It's practically the first thing Basia has said since we met her. She's really shy. Hopefully, this is progress and it means that she's opening up.

"Okay," I say, doing my best to sound neutral. "Did she teach you?" I ask Lottie.

"Kind of. Yeah," Lottie says. "She's helped me learn how to handle the dreams instead of push them away. The more I let Mom come to me, the more she does."

"Interesting," I say. "And Mom flat out told you about Puck in a dream? Like, his name and everything?"

"Not his name, no," Lottie confirms, kicking one foot as it dangles off the sofa. "But she told me we had a brother… That she had a son…"

"Wow," I say.

"That's why I looked funny when you told me. I was surprised, but not surprised at the same time. I'm still a newbie when it comes to psychic powers. I guess I still don't trust myself. Not like Basia does. She's really good."

Lottie smiles at Basia, then leans over to kiss her on the lips.

"I'm officially impressed," I say, nodding my approval.

I've never been one to buy into things like psychic powers, but I won't discount them either. Who am I to say what's real and what's not? Besides, my own dream about Mom tends to make me believe things can happen that are beyond our ability to rationalize. Whether you call them psychic powers, supernatural occurrences, or miracles, I aim to keep my mind open.

"Really?" Lottie asks. "You don't think we're crazy?"

She seems excited, eager for my approval.

"Who am I to judge?" I ask. "I had a dream about Mom during a nap yesterday, and it seemed real. It felt like I really communicated with her."

Lottie sits up straight, scooting to the edge of the sofa. I sit down in an armchair nearby. I like the close physical proximity. Maybe we're finally getting somewhere.

"Tell me about it," she says.

I do. I describe how exhausted I was after the red eye flight and Grandpa's death, and how Rags took such good care of me, getting me into his guest room for a nap while he washed my clothes and cooked me dinner. Lottie smiles when I talk about Rags. I get the idea she really likes him. I'm so glad. Maybe he can be like a big brother to her. I explain the details of the dream, describing how Mom looked and how we were on the beach near our old house on Kestrel Cay. We lived in that house when Lottie was born. I imagine it holds a special place in her heart like it does in mine. By the time I tell her about Mom telling me she's sorry, Lottie's face is wet with tears. Finally, we're connecting. *Really* connecting.

"I miss her every day," Lottie sniffles. "Do you, Margot? Do you miss her?"

"Absolutely. I do," I confirm. "I miss her terribly."

"Are you mad at her for having another child we didn't know about back then… when she was still alive?"

I consider the question. I am mad at Mom for that. Sort of. But I'm also happy to have Puck as a brother and Herbert as a grandfather. I'm happy that my circle has expanded. And besides, what's done is done.

"A little," I admit. "How about you?"

"Same," she says. "I wonder why she didn't tell us, which makes me wonder what else she didn't tell us."

I nod knowingly. Lottie and I understand each other. It suddenly strikes me that even though our experiences of Mom's death and the aftermath are different, we're still the only two people in the world who had Annie and Jon Callaway for parents. The only two who had Mari for a dog and Vern for a grandpa, and we're the only two who lived as siblings in the house on Kestrel Cay. We are intrinsically bonded for life, whether we try to pretend otherwise or not.

"Right," I say. "I've wondered that, too."

Lottie leans further towards me, practically grabbing my hand that sits on the arm of my chair.

"Hey," she whispers, as if she's going to talk about something secret that only the two of us know. "Do you think Cap looks like Mari?"

I smile broadly, joy overtaking my face. Basia smiles, too, seemingly proud that she could help loosen Lottie up and get her talking to me.

"Yes!" I reply. "I was telling Rags about her yesterday, and she was with Mom in my dream. Good ol' Marina. She was the best girl. The dog that defined our childhoods. I'm certain she thinks she helped raise us."

"Do you remember the way she used to sneak onto the foot of one of our beds after Mom went to sleep?"

"I do," I confirm. "Mari was smart. She waited to hear Mom's bedroom door close for the night, then she'd slink into one of our rooms. She knew we'd let her up on the bed. She probably knew to jump down when she heard Mom's door open again in the morning."

"Mari had no shame," Lottie says, chuckling. "And it was the same when we'd feed her under the table. Do you remember that, too?"

"Oh, yeah, I do. Grilled cheese was her favorite. You think Mom knew how much we fed that dog?"

Lottie laughs now, her guard down. It's glorious. I can't wait for Rags to see how different she is without the sour edge. I want this version of Lottie in my life. I want this kind of easy sibling relationship. I didn't think it was possible, but I'm feeling it now.

"Surely, she did," I say. "Unless she thought we were a couple of little piggies."

We laugh together, the memories warm in our hearts and minds. As I glance around Heron Cottage, I'm overwhelmed by my good fortune. There's sadness and loss, for sure, but there's also grace and beauty. I wish I hadn't stayed away all these years. I see now that I didn't have to. I could have been here, on Hideaway Isle, to watch my little sister grow up. Not to mention, I could have spent much more time with Grandpa Vern and my best friend, Chevelle. Maybe I could have met Puck and Herbert sooner and developed a bond with them while Herbert's wife, Mildred, was still alive. Tears spring to my eyes as I think about what might have been.

Lottie takes my hand. It's the first time we've touched. A flood of emotion washes over me, along with visceral memories of our shared past. It's all there, just below the surface. I begin to sob as I remember special times my sister and I had together. I hold onto her hand tightly as I allow the images to come rushing back.

I can see Lottie as a toddler, asking me to braid her hair, her rosy cheeks plump and dewy. I remember the feel of her silky locks between my fingers, her little back against my legs. She was trusting then. She hadn't been hurt or abandoned, and she thought life would turn out for the best. She had a glimmer in her eyes, a spring in her step, and a smile fixed on her cute little face. I took being her big sister for granted back then. I never thought we'd grow apart. Never thought we'd lose each other. I'm so incredibly grateful that we've found our way back.

"It's okay, Margot," Lottie says, patting my hand. "I promise. It's okay."

I dab at my eyes.

"You shouldn't be the one reassuring me," I say through tears. "I'm the one who is supposed to take care of you. And I've failed you, Lottie. I really am so very sorry. Can you ever forgive me?"

Her eyes are wet with tears, but my sister has a quiet strength about her. Perhaps I've underestimated her character. Big time. It seems that Lottie's hard, explosive exterior is protective. Underneath, she's as sensitive and sweet as she ever was. I see that now.

"It's going to be okay," she says. "*We* are going to be okay."

The tears continue to flow. They're happy tears and sad tears, coexisting the same as the happiness and sadness in our hearts. Letting some emotion out is cathartic. I feel closer to Lottie than I have in as long as I can remember. I'm so relieved. And happy. I'm overwhelmed by just how much.

Lottie and I are still sitting together, hand in hand, when we hear someone at the front door.

25

COME KNOCKING

"Is that them already?" Lottie asks, a look of concern on her face.

I'm glad to see the concern. I want my little sister to be more cautious.

"Probably," I say. "Chevelle said when I texted her that she was already with Puck. They were going to pick Herbert up and head over."

"Herbert?" Basia asks.

"Our... other grandpa," I say, gesturing to Lottie. "Puck's grandpa. And Annie's father."

"I thought your mom's parents died when she was a child," Basia says.

"That's what we were told," I confirm. "Apparently not, though."

Lottie seems eager to meet our new bonus family members. She leaps to her feet and rushes to the front door, her long hair bouncing behind her. My sister is all smiles, her face alight. Her hand is on the chain, removing it, when I stop her.

"Wait!" I say. "We need to be sure it's them. Check the peephole."

No windows face the front porch in this house since it's deep, front to back, instead of wide, side to side. Our only vantage point to see who is at the door is through the peephole. Lottie stands on her toes to look. She's several inches shorter than me. I expected her to have grown taller by now, but I'm adjusting to the way she is. I wouldn't change a thing. Her adult form is still new to me, though.

"I can't see anything," she says. "Just blackness. Is something wrong with this peephole?"

"I don't know," I say. "But I wouldn't think so. Rags seems to keep things in tip-top shape. Do you see a fisheye lens in the hole? It should allow a wider view."

"It's completely black," Lottie confirms.

I stiffen, my senses alert. It doesn't sound like Rags to have blacked out the only view of the front porch. The hair on the back of my neck stands up. Something isn't right.

"Did they even knock?" I ask. "Or did we just hear someone out there? I don't remember a knock. Or a bell."

Basia sits up straight now, becoming alarmed. I admire her good sense. She seems more worldly than my sister. More street savvy and conscientious about her surroundings. Maybe that's due to a past that necessitated it. I don't wish a difficult history on her, but Lottie could certainly benefit from someone who can keep her grounded. My sister seems to be a dreamer with her head mostly in the clouds. That's all well and good, but she needs a partner who will provide balance.

"I didn't hear a knock or a bell," Basia confirms.

Before she can finish her sentence, we hear a loud clunking sound on the back porch.

"That isn't Puck and Chevelle," I say. "They'd go to the front door."

"Margot, I'm scared," Lottie whimpers, racing to my side.

"It's okay," I lie. "We can handle this."

Basia looks at me, terror in her eyes as we hear the unmistakable sound of a cordless drill. They're drilling through the locks on the door handle and deadbolt. I'm sure of it. There's a chain on the front door, but I don't remember noticing if there was also one on the back. It matters very little, anyway. These people are determined to get in. It won't take them long to do it.

"What's that?" Lottie asks urgently. Then, when I don't respond right away, "Margot, what is that sound? Please. Tell me."

"It's a power drill. They're breaking through the locks."

"Shit," Basia says.

Lottie appears suddenly speechless. She's gripping my arm so tightly my hand is turning blue. It's time for me to spring into action. I wish Rags was here to take the lead. He's trained for this. I'm not, but I'm trained better than Lottie or Basia are for it. I tell myself to think fast. No one friendly would be blacking out the peephole and drilling through the locks. I scour my memory, trying to figure out how they might have found us. It must be the same guys who killed Vern and those cops. Who else could it be? It's them. But how?

"Did you tell anyone you were here today?" I ask

Lottie and Basia.

They shake their heads.

"No," Basia says. "We've been with you the whole time. You've witnessed what we've done since we ran into you at the campground. We haven't seen or spoken to anyone."

Basia rushes toward us, clinging to my other side and biting her nails. They're both shaking like leaves. I look down at my hands and realize that I am, too.

"Are you sure?" I ask. "You didn't text anyone?"

More banging sounds loudly from the back of the cottage. We can't see the door from where we're standing, but it's obvious that whoever is out there is serious about getting in. We don't have much time.

"No," Lottie says, finding her voice. "I swear, Margot. You can check my phone if you want. I didn't text anyone…"

My sister's eyes suddenly widen as if something has occurred to her.

"What is it?" Basia asks.

My stomach drops. I swear, if Lottie gave away our location, I'll kill her myself.

"I… I didn't think about it at the time… but…" Lottie stammers.

I shoot her a look that says she had better spill. Now.

"What did you do?" I ask.

Glass shatters in the distance. I didn't pay enough attention to the layout of the back of the cottage. I don't know exactly where the sound is coming from. I *think* there was glass in the top half of the door that leads into the kitchen from the screened porch. They're getting close.

"The selfie…" Lottie mumbles. "I posted it to my social media. I might have had location services turned on. I'm so sorry, Margot. I was just feeling happy and I wanted to share. Posting selfies to social media is a habit. I didn't think anything of it…"

I shake my head and close my eyes. I'm furious. Lottie is such a liability. Her carelessness has caused one problem after another. Now, it may cost us our lives. If trained police officers weren't able to defend themselves against these guys, how will we? I fear it may be over for us. What a terrible shame. My life is just now blossoming into everything I've ever wanted it to be. I have more of a future than ever before. I fear that future is about to be taken away, Lottie and me victim to untimely deaths as our parents and other family members. I wonder if the Callaways are cursed. I don't see a way out.

Clamoring noises again ring out from the back of the house and I can tell there's more than one person there. They aren't even trying to hide their presence. Like yesterday morning at Grandpa Vern's house, these guys are bold. They don't seem to care who hears or sees them. They've nearly made it all the way inside. If I'm going to fight for our lives, it's now or never.

Determination buoying me, I decide to give it my all. The Navy never prepared me for hand to hand combat like they did Rags, but they did send me to survival training. I've been taught to keep my wits about me in a life or death situation. It's time to put everything I've learned to use.

My senses heightened, I begin to think strategically.

"Lottie, call 9-1-1," I instruct.

I doubt there's time for first responders to get here

and I doubt their ability to help even if they do, but it's worth a try at this point.

"Basia, you find a place to hide," I say.

She digs her heels in.

"I'm not going anywhere without Lottie," she says.

Lottie's face lights up in response to Basia's stance, but then it falls when she realizes her phone isn't working. She tries to dial 9-1-1 repeatedly, but there's no signal.

"It's dead," she says. "There's no reception."

Basia pulls her phone out and tries it, but it's dead, too.

"Nothing for me either," she adds.

I don't bother checking mine. I know it's the same.

"They're using a jammer," I say. "Look, the two of you need to hide. Right now."

"Did they use a jammer at Grandpa Vern's?" Lottie asks.

"I don't know," I reply. "We're out of time, Lottie. Hide somewhere they won't find you. If you can escape out a window or a crawlspace… Any way out, you take it. Then go get help."

Lottie protests.

"We can't leave you out here alone, Margot. I just got you back… I… I can't lose you again. I won't."

My sister practically bawls as she says the words. Even though I was angry with her a few minutes ago, now I want to protect her at all costs. She's weak and vulnerable. She isn't as tough as I am. Life hasn't yet made her hard. I don't want it to.

I shove her towards Basia.

"Get my sister out of here," I say. "There's no more time. I have to figure out my next move."

Basia looks at me, comprehending but lacking the gumption to move.

"Go!" I shout. "Go now!"

Lottie cries for me as Basia drags her out of the room and up the stairs. It's gut wrenching to see her so upset and torn away. It reminds me of the day of Mom's accident when Lottie came completely apart. I see it clearly in my mind as if it was yesterday. I can practically smell the blood and hear the sirens, my body ice cold even though it was over ninety degrees outside, my eyes registering the sights in front of me but my mind not processing them as real. If I'm honest with myself, seeing Lottie so upset was worse than seeing Mom's body so mangled. Even though it was traumatic to see Mom that way, I knew on a fundamental level that she was already gone and no longer suffering. Lottie, on the other hand, was suffering terribly. Worse than I was. I wanted to help her, but didn't know how. It was my own failure that sent me away. My shame at not being able to come through for my sister was the catalyst that set me on the run. Now, it feels like a repeat of the same experience. We're suffering, and I can't help Lottie despite how much I want to. This is my worst nightmare.

I shake my head as if to shake off the traumatic memory. I force myself to focus. To remember my military training. Maybe I shouldn't have run from Hideaway Isle all those years ago, but the fact is, I learned a lot during my time away. I hear the intruders break through the door, their footsteps heavy on the hardwood floors inside the cottage. Under the threat of imminent danger, I reaffirm my choice to fight with everything I have. For myself, for my future with Rags, for my sister, and for my mom, dad, and grandpa who would be here to protect us if they could.

With Lottie and Basia out of sight, I look for a place to hide myself until I can come up with a plan. I'm at a disadvantage because I don't know the layout of the cottage, but I'll have to make do. It isn't a huge property, so the layout ought to be predictable. Moving quickly, I scurry into a den on the main level. There's a large desk in the room, so I use it to barricade the door. My pulse races as I heave, using all of my strength to get the heavy piece of furniture in place. I know it won't hold them for long. Every minute I can gain is another chance for survival. I hope that Rags might show up and help, but I know I can't count on it. Our survival lies squarely in my hands.

I pick up the landline phone on the desk, but as expected, the line is dead. Silence greets me and I hastily put the receiver back down, careful not to make noise. I try the desktop computer, too, but it shows no internet signal. There's a window in the room. I try it, but it appears to have been nailed shut. I instantly learn that it's no use, anyway, because a burly bald guy wearing a black leather jacket and holding a pistol is standing outside, a few feet away. He turns towards me, but I duck just in time. So much for that plan. I won't be able to escape out the window. Most likely, Lottie and Basia won't be able to, either. I move on, scanning my knowledge bank for something that will help me figure out what to do.

I think about the black duffel bag that Rags had, and I try to remember where he left it. He had extra weapons in there. If I could find the bag, there would be enough firepower to go up against these guys with a decent chance of coming out the victor. I know how to shoot. I shot expert on my first day of training at the Naval Academy. I can handle myself in that regard. But I don't remember Rags taking the duffel bag out of the Subaru. He wouldn't have wanted to spook Lottie and Basia. They don't know he was a Navy SEAL. They might have been uncomfortable with loaded weapons. *Damn.* So much for that plan. Rags has the Subaru with him at the burger joint. I'll have to try another tactic.

My palms sweat as I hear the guys searching the house. They seem to be looking for something again, just like Rags suspected. I hear glass being smashed, drawers and cupboards in the kitchen being slammed, and more heavy stomping feet. I've got to hide. There's no other way. Since they haven't come for me in this room first, maybe they didn't hear me moving the desk. Maybe they don't know I'm here yet. There's no vehicle parked outside. Maybe they think the cottage is empty. If I can somehow hide long enough to surprise them when I'm ready with a plan, that's my biggest advantage right now.

I scan the room for a good spot to hide. I must find a place. Under the desk won't work. It's too exposed. The only other pieces of furniture are armchairs and a daybed. I consider the daybed, eyeing it as the possibilities tumble through my mind. There might be enough room for me to squeeze in under the mattress and remain hidden until the guys leave. The biggest problem is the fact that I'd be trapped there, unable to gain a good vantage point or escape. No, that won't work. I have to come up with something else, and fast.

For the first time, I notice a closet in one corner of the

room, close to the window. A closet is probably too
obvious as a place to hide, but I decide to check it out
anyway. I slink over, careful not to be seen through the
window, then I look inside. It's mostly empty except for
some cleaning supplies and a few boxes of knick knacks
pushed against the back wall. I fume, out of options. But
then something strikes me. I suddenly find it odd that
there are boxes of knick knacks here when that's the
name of Chevelle's car. Maybe it's a sign.

I rummage through the boxes, all left open on the top.
I don't see anything remarkable inside. It looks like these
items might have been on the trio of tall shelves I saw in
the den. Perhaps Rags decided to add more books,
displacing these decorative items. If this is a sign of some
kind, I need to figure out what it means soon. They'll find
me if I stay here. I again think about the dream with
Mom and how insistent she was in saying she was sorry. I
wonder what in the world this means. I tell myself to
think fast. To let whatever can help me get out of this
alive come forth and reveal itself. It's now or never.

I ball my hand up into a fist and fling it in frustration.
I'm at the end of my rope. Until something miraculous
happens. The swing of my fist causes one of the boxes to
tip. I catch it before it hits the floor and thus prevent any
loud noise, but when the box moves, I notice a square
access door in the wall behind it. It must go to a
crawlspace or attic. My anticipation builds as I realize I
can fit through the door, and I can pull the stack of boxes
flush up against it, obscuring the door from view.
Hopefully, I can remain hidden that way. Maybe we
actually have a chance.

26

DEAR LIFE

My heart pounds hard against my ribs as I look and listen through a vent grate in one wall of the living room. I'm hyper focused. The opening is tiny, but it's enough for me to see and hear what's happening without being detected. That is, if I can slow my breathing. I decide to watch for a while to see what I can learn before making a move.

I managed to get into the crawl space through the access door I found in the den. I doubt newer homes would have this kind of infrastructure, so I'm thanking my lucky stars that this old home does. To my pleasant surprise, a box of tools greeted me when I entered the bowels of the cottage. I now have several items at my disposal, including a hand saw, a couple of hammers with nails, and a cordless drill. It isn't much, but it's something. I replaced the door behind me and think I'm actually hidden. Now I have the tactical advantage.

From what I can tell, there are at least three men on the property. There's the one I saw outside who appears to be a brute, hired for his size. I doubt he's the brains of the operation. There are two others inside the cottage. One is rummaging through the kitchen while the other searches the living room. Neither of them strike me as leaders, either. They're big, too, and are wearing the same black leather jackets, but they're not as big as the guy outside. They're definitely looking for something. I wrack my brain, but can't imagine what. In fact, I can't come up with any connection between Grandpa Vern's condo and the two properties Rags owns. What do these guys see as the common thread? The only link I can find is me. I wonder if they've been to Lottie's place.

"Nothing," the dark-skinned guy searching the living room says.

He seems to be taking the lead. He also appears to be the smartest of the three.

"What now?" the guy from the kitchen calls back. "You gonna call the boss? He wanted to show up on site if we found anything useful."

"He told me the same," the living room guy replies. "I'm not ready to give up. Let's check upstairs again."

My stomach drops. The word *again* is of particular concern. That means Lottie and Basia stayed successfully hidden the first time these guys searched near them. This go 'round, I expect they'll search more thoroughly. I'm terrified for my sister. I find it interesting that their boss is in close enough proximity to want to come here in person. Maybe he doesn't trust these guys to deliver whatever it is he wants them to find. Or worse, I wonder if the boss expects his guys to capture someone he wants them to question. The thought sends a wave of nausea bounding through my body like a tsunami. All at once, the situation becomes clear in my mind. It's happening, and I'm helpless to stop it.

The light-skinned man from the kitchen races upstairs with an impressive swiftness, catching Lottie and Basia off guard. I hear my sister scream. It's a blood curdling scream, reminiscent of sounds from the National Geographic Channel of prey being snatched by a predator it knows will end its life. I want to go to her. To save her. But I can't. Not yet. These guys are armed. I don't stand a chance if I rush in without a plan.

"Got something good," the man calls down to his cohort as he drags Lottie by the hair.

He's being rough with her. It's probably intentional, so she'll be intimidated and afraid. She's thrashing like an animal caught in a trap, screaming bloody murder. I have a clear view of her when she and the man pulling her get to the bottom of the stairs. *Oh, Lottie.* It pains me to see my sister like this. The man pulls a chair out from the dining table and slings Lottie into it. He pulls a wad of zip ties out of his jacket pocket and binds her wrists and ankles, shackling her to the chair as she continues to scream. Her voice is shrill, panicked. It hardly sounds like her. Basia doesn't emerge from upstairs. I wonder where she is and if she somehow found a way out.

"You calling him, or should I?" the dark-skinned man asks, a shit-eating grin on his face.

His callous demeanor makes me physically ill. These guys act like cats toying with a mouse. The more Lottie squirms and cries, the more excited they seem to get. They haven't gagged her yet. They're allowing her to scream her head off as if they enjoy watching her distress.

"Let's figure out who we have here," the man nearest Lottie says.

"Do it."

"Alright, little girl," he says, taking a cigar cutter out of his pocket. He grabs Lottie's fingers where they're tied behind her back and slips the cutter over one. "You're going to tell us your real name, or you lose a finger. Got that?"

Lottie nods, desperate. She doesn't see any other option. I don't either. The cigar cutter will take her finger clean off in a matter of seconds.

"Go ahead, then. What's your name?"

She doesn't hesitate.

"Lottie Callaway," she announces through tears.

"Jackpot," the dark-skinned man says. "I'm calling it in. Boss will want to get here right away."

"Hell, yeah, he will," the other man shouts. "This is the little rich girl from the boat tour company. And now she's going to give us the rest of her money. There has to be more where that came from."

I'm floored as I piece the scraps of information together. Is that all this is about? Some opportunists who heard about the boat tour accident when it was in the news and decided Lottie was a source of money. I guess they weren't wrong. And I suppose the news coverage that listed my sister as owner of the company at age nineteen would be enough to tip off slimeballs looking for an easy payday. At nineteen, few people would have had the wherewithal to make that kind of money themselves. It's pretty obvious that it must have come from family, either financed by a wealthy relative or a result of inheritance that came from one. Either way, you have a kid with money. An easy target for extortion. I guess Grandpa Vern was collateral damage. Or else they figured he was the source of Lottie's wealth. Again, they weren't wrong.

Poor Grandpa. This confirms that his tragic death was a result of Lottie's carelessness. He spent most of his adult life sitting on the fortune his parents had given him, making sure to maintain a low profile and a middle class lifestyle, only to have his life cut short over the money he'd kept hidden. How incredibly sad. My heart hurts for Grandpa even more now that I know the motive behind his killing. These guys are probably looking for information that will help them to the rest of Lottie's money, and that of her family members.

I can't even bring myself to be mad at Lottie anymore. Not now, given the position she's in. She's suffering enough, karma apparently taking its due. I just want this to be over. I want the police to arrest these guys and their boss so we can move forward. If only my loved ones and I can get out of this alive.

The dark-skinned man speaks to their boss on the phone, saying few words, but making assurances that they'll keep Lottie restrained until he arrives. Lottie screams in response. She isn't losing her strength yet. I have to admire her feisty spirit.

For what feels like an eternity, I watch and I wait. I'm acutely aware that I'll have at least one additional man to contend with once the boss arrives. Yet my instincts tell me to stay hidden for now. Maybe it's curiosity about who this boss is. Maybe I want to solve the mystery, seeing it through to its end. I stay put, but I make my plans.

The light-skinned man tending Lottie has set his gun down on the dining table where it rests more than arm's length away. He doesn't think anyone else is here. They've searched the house twice. Lottie is tied up. He feels secure. That's evident by his relaxed posture and his glib expression. He thinks he's in charge, free to do as he wishes. He doesn't yet know that I intend to stop him cold in his tracks. By the time this is over, I aim to make him sorry he dared tangle with the Callaway sisters.

I decide my best move is to wait for the right opportunity, then leap out, surprising the men and grabbing the gun from the table. I'll have to be precise once I get the weapon so that I put a bullet in each one of them before they can react and take me out first. It's risky. Using the hand saw I have at my disposal, I'll need to cut through the drywall in an inconspicuous spot that goes unnoticed, yet affords me the right proximity to the gun. One false move on my part and Lottie and I are both done for.

I determine the best spot, then stealthily move myself into position behind a pantry door that is swung open against a wall in the dining room. Each time the men shuffle or speak, I cut a tiny section of the drywall with the handsaw. By the time I hear the boss' vehicle out front, I have nearly three quarters of the hole sliced out. I can tell it's a truck with a loud engine and not Rags' Subaru. When the men turn their attention towards the door, I finish the job. Just as I planned, I've created a hole behind the door large enough for me to emerge through when I make my move. So far, my presence hasn't been detected by anyone. Not even Lottie.

"Good work, my friends," a man's voice booms from the front of the house. "I'm very pleased."

Lottie moans in fear, seemingly unable to help herself.

It's excruciating to hear. She probably thinks her time has run out. She might be right, though not if I can help it.

"We've got her all ready for you," the light-skinned man says to his boss. "She talks. Easy. Little rich bitch means a big payday."

He says it in a sing-songy voice, making a total mockery of Lottie's dignity. I shudder. I've come to dislike this man the most. He's so pompous about the whole thing. At least, the dark-skinned man seems to have a certain reverence for what he's doing and how it affects Lottie. He's doing what he must, but he isn't taking as much glee in it.

"Yes, I see," the boss says, suddenly coming into view.

He's a short, chubby man with a red face and wavy black hair that's been dyed platinum blonde. You can see the ample dark roots forcing their way upward. He's older than the other guys, and significantly older than us. If I had to guess, I'd say he's probably around our parents' age. He turns, and I get a glimpse of his profile. All of a sudden, I realize that I know this man.

My eyes widen and my pulse quickens as I work to place him. It only takes me a minute.

It's Llew Brackus. He was a friend of Mom's the year we lived in Miami. I remember it clearly now. He visited her often at our condo in Coral Gables. He looks mostly the same, only he didn't have the bottle blonde dye job back then. He was friendly to us. Thinking about it now through the lens of my adult sensibilities, he and Mom must have been dating. They spent an awful lot of time together.

What in the hell is Llew doing *here*? As the boss of the goons who have killed multiple people and are threatening to do the same to Lottie? It doesn't add up. What cruel twist of fate would return him to our lives like this?

I shake my head and rub my temples.

Life, I think. *Why is this man here, threatening us? Please, help me understand. Help me find a way to safety.*

27

FLOCK TOGETHER

His smug voice brings me back to the present moment.

"Little Miss Callaway," Llew says to my sister, a smirk on his face. "You're all grown up."

Lottie finds her strength again, screaming as loud as she can. She doesn't seem to recognize Llew. She was twelve when he was a part of Mom's life. It might take time, but it ought to come back to her.

"Now, now," he continues, chewing on something inside of his fat lips. "No need to pierce our eardrums, my dear. We have business to tend to."

"I don't know what you're talking about!" Lottie shouts. "I don't have business with you."

Llew pulls out a chair and sits next to her, then laces his plump fingers together on the table.

"Oh, but you do," he replies. "Or should I say, your mother does."

Lottie's face crumples. "You're wrong. My mother is dead."

Llew laughs, tipping his head back and stressing the joints of the chair. He smells like cigarette smoke. I can identify the stench from my spot in the crawlspace. It's disgusting.

"I know. But she owed me a lot of money when she died. You're going to pay it back. With interest."

Now it's my face that crumples. I remember my dream about Mom and how she insisted she was so sorry. Could what Llew is saying be true? I think back about the timing of Mom's life, taking into consideration that she apparently abandoned Puck before she met Dad and had us. After Dad died, I know we struggled financially without his income. And Grandpa Vern never told us he was wealthy until the day Mom was killed. Is it possible Mom got herself into financial trouble trying to make ends meet? Did she know about the money Grandpa inherited from his parents? With these new pieces of the puzzle, an entirely different picture of Annie Callaway-- previously Annie Finley and Annie Reed-- emerges. It isn't a flattering one.

Llew signals to the light-skinned man, who steps closer to Lottie and pulls a thick black pouch from the inside pocket of his jacket then lays it on the table. He unfolds the sides, exposing a variety of shiny tools that appear to be used for torture.

"No!" Lottie shouts. "I don't know what my mom did, but she's dead and gone. I don't owe you anything."

"But you do..." Llew says. He doesn't wait for her to answer. "We can do this the easy way or the hard way."

"No!" Lottie howls again. "Leave me alone. Please. I don't have money, anyway. I was in a business that went bad."

All three of the men chuckle, apparently amused by Lottie's protests. I'm not sure how much more of this I can take. It's almost time to make my move. I begin to calculate my steps. The gun remains on the table a few feet away from anyone's reach. Llew, too, thinks they're alone. I still have the element of surprise. It's a huge advantage.

"We know all about your business, little dear," Llew says. "It's how we learned that you had money in the first place. Not many teenagers own companies like the boat tour operation so don't try to convince me you're poor. I'm quite glad that accident happened. I thought Annie's debt to me would go unpaid. But now, I'm about to come into a windfall, thanks to you."

Lottie shakes her head, apparently speechless.

"So, tell me where all of your money is held," Llew says. "If you cooperate, you won't suffer. If you don't, well, Sid here will make use of his tools."

Now we know the guy's name. I suppose that will help if my surprise attack is successful and we can turn him in to the police. Sid smiles mischievously, looking as if he can hardly wait for the chance to torture my delicate little sister. I'm completely disgusted. What makes people so evil? I tremble to think what would happen if I wasn't here to intervene.

Deciding it's time, I steel myself and prepare to take my shot. Whatever Mom did or didn't do, whether she had some secret life we didn't know about and a large debt to Llew, it doesn't matter now. What matters is saving my little sister. And saving myself.

The time has come.

I outline the steps in my mind, square up, and burst

out of the hole I've cut like a sprinter off the starting block. I push the pantry door closed, blowing past it on my way to the table and the gun. I don't bother to gauge the reactions of the people in the room. There's no time. I move through the air in a smooth, fluid motion, the adrenaline coursing through my veins providing added lift. In a few steps, I'm there. Llew and his men are too startled to react, just like I hoped.

I grab the gun and place my finger firmly on the trigger. I take Sid out first with three shots to the chest. He falls backward, a look of bewilderment on his face. Expertly, I turn to the dark-skinned man and take another few shots, hitting him in the chest, too. He stumbles, landing on the floor. Two down.

Ignoring Lottie's cries of terror, I turn the gun on Llew. He wears a look of recognition on his face. I take my shots, hitting him in the gut. He clutches the wound, his eyes wide as saucers as blood pours from his body. I scold myself for hitting him lower than the others, but there's still time to finish the job. I take aim, but I hesitate. Llew is disabled now. He doesn't have a weapon. I can see both of his hands. If I turn him in to the police, maybe it will somehow help. He might be a bad guy who would confess to other unsolved crimes. If I'm honest with myself, I'm hesitating because he was Mom's friend. If she were here, she might want him to live.

Suddenly, I feel an arm around my neck and I'm thrown to the ground. I know in an instant that it's the big man I saw outside the window. *Damn him.* He was on my radar, but I wasn't fast enough. I knew he'd come running the minute he heard shots fired. I struggle, still maintaining my grip on the gun, but I can't get my hands turned around to point it at him. He has a weapon, too, and it's pressed painfully into my back.

"Boss, should I shoot her?" he asks, his voice strained.

Llew just stares. I don't know if he's emotionally shocked by me surprising him like that, or if he's already lost enough blood that his body is going into physical shock. He claws at his gut, trying to hold everything in.

I use all of my strength to break free of the brute's hold. He's way too strong. I try mightily, but I'm immobilized. He has me at a huge disadvantage. My heart sinks. This may be the end for us.

"Margot!" Lottie cries.

"Lottie," I shout back. "Scoot yourself and try to get away. Go!"

She wriggles furiously, but only succeeds in toppling herself along with the chair she's tied to.

"It's no use," she cries.

My heart breaks. This is it.

"Boss?" the big man says. "I'm gonna shoot her. Just say the word."

I close my eyes, certain this is the end. One word, one nod even, from Llew and I'm a goner. Lottie will never get away on her own. They'll torture and then shoot her, too, once they get at her money. How sorrowful to face the end of my life knowing I'm being killed for money. Greed. Gluttony. It's sickening. I'm devastated that there isn't better than this. That Life doesn't see fit to save us.

The next thing I know, someone explodes through the front door. The man holding me down is suddenly ripped away. It's Rags. Oh, my God, I am so happy to see him. Cap swoops in behind, barking fiercely.

"Rags! Cap!" I exclaim. "You're just in time. I think I

killed two of them, and Llew here is on his way out. If you'd be a dear and finish off this last one, I'd appreciate it."

I chuckle, proud of myself for bringing humor to this life or death situation. I'm still on the floor, but I don't bother to get up. I'm not sure my legs are steady enough to hold me. Rags nods, a look of grave concern on his face.

"You're okay, then?" he asks.

"Fine," I reply. "Just a little shaken up."

Rags has the man incapacitated, tied and bound with his own leather jacket. He moved so quickly, I didn't even see how he did it. I'll have to ask when there's more time to sit around chatting. He has a gun in his hand and holds it against the man's temple.

"Does this guy get to live?" he asks.

Before I can answer, we hear the sound of sirens screaming towards us. It sounds like a whole slew of them. Probably cops and EMTs. Basia bursts in the front door looking haggard, but determined.

"I got us help!" she shouts. "I made it onto the roof, then down and over to a neighbor's house. We called for help. They're coming."

"Good girl," I say.

Basia sees Lottie on the floor and runs to her.

Llew is clearly not a threat anymore. In fact, his head is slumped and he's bleeding out. If he doesn't get medical attention soon, he won't make it. Cap seems to know that, but wants to be sure he doesn't try anything. The dog stands guard, barking at Llew as he watches the life drain from the man's body.

"Lottie, my love," Basia says, helping stand her chair

upright again and beginning to loosen the ties. "Are you alright? I was so worried about you. It felt like an eternity we were apart. I didn't know what was happening. I heard you scream..."

Lottie kisses Basia's face, tears soaking her own.

"I'm okay. Margot saved me. My big sister... She saved us all. We're all okay," Lottie proclaims.

For the first time in a long time, I know she's right. We really are all okay. It's the very best feeling. I'm proud of myself for taking the needed action to turn the tables and put an end to the hunt that had us fearing for our lives. We can move forward now, sure in the knowledge that we made it, and we'll continue to do so every day, together.

Within a few short minutes, Tom arrives and praises my smart handling of the situation we faced. He tells Rags and me that we make a great team, to which we reply-- with a shared glance and a wink-- that we already knew just how great we are together. Llew and the big brute of a man are taken by ambulance. Tom assures us they'll be prosecuted swiftly and won't pose any additional threat. Rags and I thank him and settle in on the sofa for the inevitable questioning to come. We don't mind. We're just glad to be seated next to each other, both living and breathing with bright futures ahead of us.

Not long after Tom's arrival, Puck, Chevelle, and Herbert show up, completely blindsided by the flurry of activity at the scene. We catch them up with a quick summary, but promise to go into much more depth later on. I can hardly wait to tell Chevelle about the knick knack connection and how it saved the day. Herbert invites Lottie, Basia, Rags, and me to a warm meal at his house once the police interviews are done. We gladly accept, and just like that, my family and I begin the first day of the rest of our lives. By sundown, we're sitting on Herbert's beautiful porch, sipping tea after a hearty home cooked meal.

Our story has only begun. There's much to plan, and even more to enjoy.

Rags and I must make arrangements for the day I'm scheduled to return to Whidbey Island. Lottie and I have to make up for the years we lost, and not to mention, we must plan and hold Grandpa Vern's funeral. Then there's Puck and Herbert, who we must get to know, along with Puck's girlfriend, Chely, and their baby boy.

I envision so many good things for our collective future. We'll grow up and grow old together, sharing laughs, silly stories from our childhoods, memories of those who have gone before, and inside jokes others can't possibly understand. We'll support each other through thick and thin, rely on each other, and be there no matter what. We'll travel together, seeing the world in each other's eyes, blissfully aware of what a gift it is to experience new places with the people we love.

All in due time as we spend each moment, each second, living this life together, my family and me.

I like the sound of that.

THE END.

―――――

Margot and Lottie Callaway, Puck Reed, Rags Bertram, Basia Guthrie, and more of your favorite characters return in the second full-length novel in The Summer Isle Series.

Get it now:

The Girl in Hideaway Park
The Summer Isle - Book Two

―――――

Read the prequel short story for free when you sign up for Kelly Utt's email newsletter.

The Boy on Sunset and Main
The Summer Isle - Prequel

ENJOY THIS BOOK?

A NOTE FROM AUTHOR KELLY UTT

Honest reviews of my books help bring them to the attention of other readers.

If you've enjoyed this book, I would be very grateful if you could spend just five minutes leaving a review (it can be as short as you like) on the book's product page where you purchased and on Goodreads or BookBub.

Thank you very much.

ABOUT THE AUTHOR

STANDARDS OF STARLIGHT BOOKS
KELLY UTT

Kelly Utt writes emotional novels for readers who enjoy both suspense and sentimentality. She was born in Youngstown, Ohio in 1976.

Kelly grew up with a dad who would read a book on a weighty topic, ask her to read it, too, and then insist they discuss it together, igniting her passion for life's big questions. That passion is often reflected inKelly's novels, giving them a depth which leaves readers wanting more and thinking about her stories long after the last lines are read.

Kelly holds a Bachelor's degree in psychology from

the University of Tennessee, Knoxville and she studied graduate-level interactive media at Quinnipiac University.

She lives in the Nashville suburb of Franklin, Tennessee with her husband and sons.

www.kellyutt.com

CPSIA information can be obtained
at www.ICGtesting.com
Printed in the USA
BVHW031149300820
587649BV00001B/429